Master of the Imagination!

Wilson Tucker, famed science fiction novelist and short story writer, has got the world on a yo-yo string. Reality loop-de-loops around his wrist. He can make time stop and retrieve it neatly. He pushes the imagination to its furthest limits and leaves it spinning.

Endlessly inventive, with a piercing wit, Tucker is a master at finding the slight permutations of reality that yield a gold mine of otherworldly adventure, space-age suspense and fantastic fun.

THE BEST OF
WILSON TUCKER

A TIMESCAPE BOOK
PUBLISHED BY POCKET BOOKS NEW YORK

Another *Original* publication of TIMESCAPE BOOKS

A Timescape Book published by
POCKET BOOKS, a Simon & Schuster division of
GULF & WESTERN CORPORATION
1230 Avenue of the Americas, New York, N.Y. 10020

ISBN: 0-671-83243-3

First Timescape Books printing February, 1982

10 9 8 7 6 5 4 3 2 1

POCKET and colophon are trademarks of Simon & Schuster.

Use of the TIMESCAPE trademark is by exclusive license
from Gregory Benford, the trademark owner.

Printed in the U.S.A.

CONTENTS

Right now, today, and for the next thirty years or so Pluto is, in effect, the eighth planet from the sun rather than the ninth. Pluto is making its perihelion passage and during the passage its orbit will bring it nearer the sun—and Earth—than at any time during the last two hundred and fifty years. This close passage offers a splendid opportunity for ships to reach Pluto from Earth bases, for the shipment of men and freight and astronomical gear, and for the erection of an automated observatory there to study planet X.

Planet X orbits in frigid darkness a hundred million miles beyond Pluto's aphelion, and there will not be another chance to see it for two and a half centuries. Go now.

TO THE TOMBAUGH STATION

Toronto: August, 2009

KATHY BRISTOL ENTERED HER SUPERVISOR'S office by the side door, slipping from the public corridor into his room without having to run the gauntlet of curious faces in the outer offices. She let herself in with her own key, and the supervisor mumbled a perfunctory greeting without glancing up from his paperwork. He said, "Umm, Kate," merely to acknowledge her presence. His desk was littered and untidy.

"Umm, Kate," she retorted. "Five or six people have keys to that door."

"But all of the others are elephants in wooden clogs. And none of the others wears perfume." He paused to sniff. "You've changed it."

"Look at me, governor."

The supervisor turned from his desk and blinked at the young woman. He blinked again. She reminded him of a tall, extroverted showgirl—the brassy, half-educated kind of girl who supposed that successful showgirls should resemble courtesans. "Umm," he said again. "You have changed." And then he noticed her hair. "I say, you've also changed your hair."

"I like change, governor."

"Yes, I expect so. Come around and sit down." He prowled over the littered desk and finally found the object of his search, which he handed across to her as she took the proffered chair. "This is your script."

"I've read the script," Kate reminded him, but she accepted the volume and thumbed through it once more.

The script consisted of nearly fifty pages of typed matter, plus numerous handwritten annotations on the margins of several pages; all were stapled together and bound with a stiff blue cover. A man's name—Irvin Webb—and his city of residence was written on the cover, together with the file number assigned to him. The bulky volume was a reasonably complete dossier on that man and his career and his vehicle. It detailed the grim case in which he was presently involved. Printed in minute type on the outside back cover of the dossier was the name and headquarters address of the Interworld Insurance Company. Several employees of the company, working under the direction of the supervisor had compiled the document. Kate Bristol had needed to read it but once to commit the contents to memory.

A colored photograph of Irvin Webb was included in the volume and she studied that photograph anew. She noted the network of harsh lines on his face and neck, and the tiny cancer scars marking his burnt skin—lines and scars that readily identified his poor profession. Irvin Webb was a sky tramp.

"He is long overdue," she said flatly.

The supervisor agreed to that. "Forty-odd, I think. Umm, yes, he's forty-three years old. Five to ten years beyond the ordinary death or retirement date, I would say. And he knows it, Kate. That certain knowledge may have pushed him over the edge."

"They seldom quit in time." She peered at the eyes in the photograph and found them black, contrasting starkly with the white or grey hair.

"Greed," the supervisor reminded her. "Or aimlessness. They always seem to believe they can find one more cargo, make one more trip. They continue to pay us expensive premiums and continue to fly to the bitter end, seldom realizing the latter affect the former. This Webb, now . . ."

"Compelling motive," the woman suggested.

"Most compelling," her supervisor nodded. "A considerable sum is involved here. With one partner dead and the other in jail—well, there you are."

"What about the one in jail?"

"Forget him. You know absolutely nothing of him."

"All right, governor." She tapped the dossier. "Irvin Webb is our prime suspect?"

"He is; otherwise the assignments would have been different." The supervisor had no compunction on the assignment; he knew the woman to be cold, efficient and tough-minded—he knew her for a huntress. And he had long ago learned, via the grapevine, that at least one man in the outer office had discovered her statuesque body was not to be played with. He said, "I expect this will be routine. For you, at any rate."

"Routine," she repeated. "Give Webb the works."

"But subtly, of course. Remember that you are only the interrogator; not the judge, nor the jury, nor the executioner. We will leave all that to the proper authorities when you have completed your examination."

"Oh, very subtly," she smiled. "He is an odd character."

"He is a deadly character, if my suspicions are correct."

Kate said thoughtfully, "It was a dirty way to die. A dirty way for anyone to die."

"It was a most unusual way," the supevisor pointed out. "Men have died before in similar fashion, quite by accident. Proven accident. Men have met death in many strange and disquieting ways, but this particular kind of death is revolting—and, just perhaps, ingenious. That is what worries me." He studied his hands on the desktop. "You must ascertain if this man—this Webb—committed murder. And if you find that he did, then you must bring me sufficient evidence to take into court." He looked up quickly at the woman's rouged face. "And I know you well enough, Kate, to know that you relish the job."

She answered him with an old cliché. "I'll hound him to the Tombaugh Station for you."

"I hope that won't be necessary," he said dryly. "Now, please, let us examine the matter of your identity." He opened a desk drawer and removed a sealed envelope. "Open it."

Kate ripped the envelope. A bankbook, a partially-used check book, a birth certificate and an I.D. card tumbled into her lap.

The supervisor said, "Read them, handle them, cover them liberally with your fingerprints. The bankbook is a record of your deposits, of course, and the checkbook will show your current balance posted in the proper place."

"How did I earn all this money?"

"In any way that suits your fancy; it is a matter which cannot be easily proven or disproven. We have assumed that a Webb-inspired investigation—if any—will not probe beyond that Omaha bank." He stared at her new appearance. "You might be an actress, you know. A rather flamboyant creature, not quite deserving top billing."

"Thank you for the flattery. Will this be enough money?"

"We believe so. You will be charged an exorbitant sum, and you should react accordingly, but this amount should be sufficient."

She stared at him. "Exorbitant? Where am I going?"

"You are going to book passage on Webb's vessel."

"But where am I going?"

"I really don't know," was the bland reply. "I wish I did. To the far moons? Titan, perhaps? To the Ice Rings? I don't know, Kate. You are going to any distant place that will require a journey of several weeks. You are going to any far moon where he may have business. You will remain with him for a considerable length of time, and that is certain to involve a flight to somewhere or other. Your objective is sufficient time to gather indisputable evidence, evidence to convince the police and the courts."

"Great Smith, governor, I said I'd hound him to the Tombaugh Station, but I didn't expect to be taken seriously. Do you know where he does business?"

"Certainly. We insure him, his vehicle and his cargo. Kate, if this man is guilty of murdering his associate for the sake of their partnership insurance, he will not simply confess overnight for your convenience. Remember that he is stubborn, and enduring. Stay with him, pry it out of him. I expect it may take considerable time."

She slapped a quick hand on the desktop. "How much is the bounty? I work for money, governor."

"Twenty percent of the principle sum involved."

"And what is the principle sum involved?"

The supervisor named a figure that caused her to whistle with surprise. "No wonder you want to show misrepresentation! The company is on the hook."

"Oh, now, it isn't too large a figure for men and machines in that trade," he said defensively. "We find these vehicles and their personnel an attractive risk."

"Except when the personnel tries to con you."

"Well said. We simply cannot allow an unjust death to masquerade as an accident. What will people think?"

"They'll think it can happen twice or a dozen times. But I won't get off the ground with these papers."

"Of course not. You did not anticipate the journey in advance; at least, not in time to secure standard clearances. Ask Webb's advice. He will tell you to buy what you need on the black market. Do so."

Kate studied the card and the certificate. "Do I really appear to be thirty-two years old?"

"Much older, I expect."

"You've been married too long, governor; you've lost the tactful touch. All right, I'm thirty-two, I have some money and I want to go barreling out across the solar system. Do you have anything more to show me?"

"Nothing more. Now you show *me*."

Kate removed her gloves and extended her hands, knowing that the supervisor wanted to see. Her skin was softly feminine with just a shade of natural tan, the skin of a well-groomed woman in her middle twenties. The man behind the desk sucked in his breath when she parted her fingers. The webbing of skin between the fingers was cracked and rotting, and seemed ready to peel away.

When the supervisor had examined the apparent affliction to his satisfaction, Kate said, "My toes are the same."

"Let me see, please."

She moved her shoes and long colored stockings to reveal her feet. There, the crowded and wrinkled skin between her toes seemed to show an advanced stage of disease.

"It seems to be an adequate job," he commented.

"It is an adequate job."

"And the remaining parts of your body?"

"Adequate," she repeated dryly.

"Sufficient to cause a man to stop and reconsider?"

"Sufficient to stop a man in his tracks unless he is blind." The huntress grinned maliciously. "Irvin Webb isn't blind."

"Well and good. And now, your radio?"

"Buried, and sending," she stated flatly.

The supervisor had the uncomfortable feeling that the woman was laughing at him. He passed his hand over an intercom panel and said, "Radio room."

A distant voice responded. "Yes, sir?"

"Are you now receiving Kate Bristol?"

"Yes, sir. A constant signal mixed with some static, but we attribute that to interference within the building. We have a fix on your office, sir."

"Very well." The supervisor broke the connection. His following sigh revealed his age and his burden. "Well, Kate, we seem to have completed your defenses, and I sincerely hope they *are* adequate. It is useless to pretend I don't worry about you. I do. But it would be equally useless to place a man on this assignment; Webb will not tolerate another man, although he may accept you because of your sex. I am hoping he will.

"Now, Kate, don't take unnecessary risks. Do nothing beyond what is needed to determine his guilt or innocence. I am prepared to accept your decision on that. If you find him innocent the company will put through the check without delay; but if you find him guilty—well, the evidence *must* convince the authorities, *must* be strong enough to give us the legal right to withhold payment. You know, of course, that a beneficiary cannot profit from murder. But whatever the outcome, the bounty will be paid you, of course."

Kate grinned. "Of course. Anything else?"

He was solemn for a moment and then asked, "Have you ever been shipwrecked? Or jettisoned?"

"No. Am I missing something?"

"If either catastrophe should occur, your life will depend on your radio," he said gravely. "Another vehicle cannot follow too closely, for it would stand revealed on his screen; your safety will depend upon how soon we can reach you from an unobserved point in space. Kate, if you go overboard for any reason, depress that panic button on the radio—it will then broadcast a continuous distress signal on several bands. With luck, someone can reach you within a week."

She grinned at the man beyond the desk. "Assuming that I am wearing a lifesuit when I go, and that the suit is stocked with provisions?"

He blinked away the levity. "Naturally. You must be prudent."

"But have you considered the possibility of me throwing *him* overboard?"

The supervisor actually smiled. "Yes, you would probably do that.This man is tough, but you would probably do that, Kate. After all, I chose you." His smile faded. "The best of hunting, Kate."

She winked at him and slipped out the private door.

Irvin Webb pulled worms from the ground and flung them to a hungry beggar.

The beggar was a young robin with speckled wings and a pale yellow belly, too young to be sensibly afraid of man. It performed a nervous, erratic dance on the lawn a scant dozen feet from the kneeling man and watched every vicious bite of the blade into the turf. There—it had happened again. Webb turned another savage scoop of earth and his fingers pulled loose a moist worm, flicking it at the hungry bird. The man stared at the ground between his knees and compared this new hole with Singleton's grave. The lawn around him was pocked with a dozen—a score of freshly dug holes and each one of them was akin to Singleton's grave.

Singleton had been in his grave since early afternoon. The funeral was a crashing bore. Webb had remembered Singleton's dream of a burial on the moon—if he ever died. Young men seldom thought of dying.

Singleton didn't get his wish, of course; he had died some twenty miles above the earth a few days ago, and had been buried six feet beneath it, in an Ontario cemetery, a few hours ago. So much for the dreams of young men. Webb jabbed the spade into the ground again and went on making still another hole.

The robin took flight in sudden alarm.

Webb heard a swift step and a woman's voice.

"Oh, hello there . . ."

Webb turned on his knees and found a woman standing before him, a very tall woman clad in some kind of opaque green fabric. She wore a wide-brimmed hat and a pair of white gloves to match. The gloves had long sleeves which reached to her elbows and beyond, disappearing beneath the sleeves of the dress. Under her large hat she had combed brown hair and a faintly pleasant if heavily made-up face. The woman looked like an actress or a whore.

"I rang," she said, "but there was no response. Perhaps you didn't hear the bell."

"It's disconnected. What do you want?"

She seemed taken aback at his attitude. "I'd like to talk to you."

"Why?"

"Well . . . on a matter of business."

"Is it important?"

"I think so." She frowned and then studied him closely. "That is, if you are Irvin Webb. Are you?"

"I'm Webb. I'm not buying anything."

"And I am not selling anything. May I talk?"

Webb looked her over more carefully and then got up to offer her a lawn chair. She *was* tall, easily matching his own spare six feet, and the tightly covered slimness of her graceful body served to emphasize it. The only square inches of naked flesh to be seen anywhere were the neck and face, and that was spoiled by the excessive cosmetics. Webb knew a sudden conviction that the woman wasn't as soft as she seemed. He outweighed her by fifty or sixty pounds, and was at least ten years older, but the conviction grew on him that she would likely hold her own in a wrestling match.

"What about the guys at the field?"

She smiled and nodded. The heavy lipstick moved awkwardly with the muscles around her mouth. "I was seeking a ship, and they said you were the only pilot available."

"Tight board," Webb agreed cryptically. "What do you want?"

"I would like to arrange a flight. A charter."

Webb had figured as much, and he also surmised that she represented money. Money was what he needed right now. That damned funeral, as cheap as it was, had taken a chunk from his meagre bank account; and those other funds he was expecting were exasperatingly slow in coming —he had never before been an insurance beneficiary, and he had no knowledge of how soon or how late they paid off.

"Sure," he said. "Where to?"

"Oh, I don't know really. Just anywhere, I guess."

"You can't just fly off into the wild blue yonder. Flights have to be plotted."

"Yes, I understand that." She paused for a moment. "Perhaps to Ganymede?"

"The far moons?" Webb shook his head in dismay. If she really wanted that the fare was as good as lost. "I've only got a can. Didn't they tell you at the field?"

"What is a can?"

"A rebuilt South Bend JB-9."

"But what is *that?*"

"A can—a bucket! A freight job with a two-man crew."

"Well?"

"Two men in the cabin—like this." He held up his two fingers closed together. "The thing is a bucket and there ain't any better name for it. The cabin sleeps two, one up on the other—the man in the top bunk sleeps with his behind rubbing the belly of the man in the bunk below. It feeds two, and you eat sitting on the floor. It carries air and water for two, if you don't breathe and drink too much. Hell, there ain't even a door on the toilet—doors make excess weight. Sister, I've got a bucket."

"But surely there is more to a ship than that. I've ridden on them."

Webb nodded sourly, staring at her extraordinary long legs and wondering why she concealed them in opaque stockings. "Sure you have. You've ridden in those fancy scows to the moon, or you've taken one of the big jobs going out. But this is a bucket! It has room for fuel and cargo, and never mind the passengers." Webb sighed and gave up the idea of a charter. "I can't cheat on fuel if I want to get somewhere and back again; I can't cheat on cargo and make money. Nobody wastes air pressure on anything outside the crew's cabin so you stay in the cabin all the time —do you follow that?"

"Of course, but—"

"No buts. You wouldn't like my bucket. Go buy a ticket to somewhere. The moon ferry will transfer you to a big job going out."

"Not this month," she contradicted him. "I asked. There is nothing scheduled for nearly four weeks."

"So wait four weeks."

"No!" She opened her purse and let him see the checkbook while she fumbled for a cigarette. "I want to go now."

"You're in a damned big hurry, sister."

"I am accustomed to doing things in a hurry."

But he neglected to answer that because a suspicion was growing in his mind. She was in too much of a hurry and the fancy scows plying the moon run weren't satisfactory to her. Why not? Webb grunted sourly. He could guess at one creasy reason why. He'd heard of it being done, and it was usually done on buckets such as his. The thing was nearly impossible to accomplish on the big scheduled ships because every passenger had to submit to a rigid physical inspection—but it could happen on a bucket like his if he wasn't careful, damned careful.

There was something to the hang of her dress, to the way she concealed her body from the sun—and from him. Her entire ensemble was simply too much of a piece and the suspicion gnawed him.

His surly glance returned to her face. "No."

She almost shouted the rebuttal. "I want to!"

"It's my bucket, sister, and I said no."

"But why not?"

Webb exploded. "I don't have to cite reasons. I don't want you." He cocked his head. "What are you running from?"

"I'm not running from anything."

"The law after you?"

"Certainly not."

"Are you one of those stupid *gafia* people? Are you an escapist? Looking for a new utopia, maybe?"

"Don't be silly. Those people aren't well."

"All right, sister, what *is* wrong with you?"

"What do you mean by that, Irvin Webb?"

"I mean just this: supposing I jumped you topside? Supposing something happened up there, something messy? What if you got sick? What if you died? How in hell could I explain that?" Webb jeered. "Go sucker somebody else. You're not going to foul my ship."

The woman was suddenly still, the small feminine movements of her body halted in rigid immobility. Webb could see the cold shock growing on her face.

She whispered, "What are you thinking?"

He said brutally, "I think you're pregnant. I think you want to jump topside and lose it."

Webb was watching her face when he should have been watching the hands—her balled fist caught him across the mouth, rocking him, and a second blow sent him sprawling among the many holes dug into the lawn.

Inside the house his radiophone buzzed.

Webb rolled on his belly and jumped to his feet, backing away. He tasted blood in his mouth and found that his teeth had torn a gash in the soft wet lining of his cheek. Now he watched her warily and knew that he had been wrong about one thing, knew the absurdity of his suspicion. She wasn't pregnant. She was holding the cloth taut across a flat stomach, daring him to repeat the accusation. Webb shrugged and admitted to himself that he was in error—this time. But it *had* been done.

"My mistake," he said curtly, nursing his lips.

"You filthy beast!"

Webb grunted and looked toward the door. The phone was calling him.

She said, "You should apologize."

Carelessly, "I apologize."

"And *mean* it!"

"Oh, go home," he shouted and walked away from her. Webb mounted the single step serving as a threshhold and entered the house, allowing the screendoor to bang noisily behind him. Striding through the empty rooms to the phone, he knew again the tomblike atmosphere of the empty house and decided to sell it, or even abandon it if he couldn't find a buyer. He was the sole occupant now.

The house, like the old freighter squatting on the field not far away, had belonged to the three of them—to Singleton, to Jimmy Cross and to himself, a partnership. But now the partnership was ripped asunder with Singleton in his grave and Cross in jail on suspicion of murder. The house and the ship would be his, all his, if Cross failed to escape a prison sentence. Webb didn't want the house.

He picked up the radiophone. "Webb here." The voice at the far end was recognized and he added, "Hello, Squirrel, what do you want with me?"

The voice told him in half a dozen rapid sentences and Webb grew excited. "The *hell* they did? After all these years!" He listened to further information and then broke in once more. "Never mind that stuff—load it on. I'll take it, Squirrel, I'll take every long ton you can cram in! Pile it on. . . . What?" A pause. "Money?"

Webb turned and squinted through the doorway. "Hell, yes, I can put up first money. Just you pack in that cargo —pinch it. I want all I can lift. And then get a plotting for me and a place on the booster. Maybe we can make it by midnight. What? Yeah, I'm coming out there now. Hang up and start working, Squirrel."

Webb dropped the phone and spun on his heel, making for the doorway. The woman was waiting where he had left her and was pretending to be interested in the many small holes in the turf. Webb grinned at the holes and again thought of Singleton in his grave.

He pushed through the door said, *"Out,* eh?"

She quickened. "You will accept my charter, Mr. Webb?"

"You want to go to the far moons?"

"I do. How much will it cost?"

Webb evaded that and asked instead, "Do you have papers?"

"Papers?"

"Flight clearances," he said impatiently. "An I.D. card,

health ticket, and so on. The guys at the field will have to seen them or you don't go topside. How about a passport?"

"I'm a North American citizen. I was born in Loveland, Ohio."

"Then you don't need a passport. The field office will issue a tourist card, but you *have* to buy a roundtrip ticket. You can't stay out there."

"How much will it cost?" she asked again.

Webb fell silent, giving the impression of weighing the matter in his mind but she knew the impression to be a false one. She watched as he examined her clothing and guessed at its price, watching him coolly estimate the sum of money she was supposed to represent. He was also studying the lines of her body beneath the clothing but she was prepared for that.

Irvin Webb was a tramp; was little different from a hundred other tramp spacemen she had seen. He was not unique. He wore his white hair cropped close in a burr cut, his skin was darkly browned and his ears were burnt black by careless—and overlong—exposure to radiation behind inadequate shielding. The tiny cancer scars she had seen on the photograph attached to the dossier now stood out prominently, even cruelly on his neck and face, contributing to his inelegance. Webb's eyes were black, and he was actually ugly—not repulsive, merely ugly. She recognized a certain brutish strength, but she knew his age as forty-three, and they both knew he was long overdue. There were no really *old* men working the skies.

He said at last, "Three thousand."

"Three—" She caught her breath and tried not to lose her temper again. The sum was staggering, despite the earlier warning from her supervisor. "I didn't expect it to be so *much*."

"You're chartering a bucket, sister, not sharing it with a dozen other people."

"But after all, three thousand!"

"Sister, the far moons are expensive. If they'd let you buy a one-way ticket I could knock down on the price, but they won't and I won't. I have to buy fuel, supplies, and a hot brick to fire the fuel. I have to buy tapes for a plotting and *then* pay for the plotting. I have to pay the booster to get me off the ground. In cash. My credit isn't worth a damn around here anymore." He spread his hands. "What's left over is my profit. I split that with my partner."

Kate was of the opinion that a considerable sum would be left over for profit, but she did not voice the opinion. "A partner? I thought it was your ship?"

"It's in my name because I'm the senior partner, but it's only half mine." He glanced at the gouged turf. "I did own a third, but the number three man died."

"Will your partner accompany us?"

"He will not. He's in jail."

"For heaven's sake! Why?"

Webb grinned crookedly. "Because the number three man died, rather suddenly."

"Oh."

"Yeah, oh. Now, there's one more piece to this deal and you have to agree to it in advance. You said you didn't care where you went so long as it was out. All right, I'll take you out. But I'm choosing the destination and I'm reserving the right to pick up and deliver cargo to that destination. You agree to that."

Kate said wistfully, "I had hoped to see Nereid. I've read so much about it and I've seen pictures of the glass caves. The interior must be a fascinating place."

"Neptune is on the other side of the sun," Webb told her flatly, "and Nereid went along with it. Only the big jobs are going out there this season." He grunted, "The interior of Nereid is just a hole in the ground and I've seen better holes. What about it?"

"Will you also provide my return passage?"

"I have to post bond for your return passage. That's regulations. If you come back with me, I collect the bond but if some other pilot brings you back he gets it."

"Three thousand?" she asked again.

"You can get a moon hop for a lot less."

"No," she said in apparent defeat, "I will pay it."

"I thought you would."

"You seem very sure of yourself, Irvin Webb."

"I am. Are you going to pay by check?"

"Of course."

"Then I'll take it now. I'm going to the field."

She stared at him stung by the implied insult. "Don't you trust anyone?"

"Yes. Me."

Webb stood before her with his feet thrust apart trying to peer through the deliberate opacity of her clothing, harshly subjecting her to an undisguised insolence of tongue and manner. Kate thought she understood the reason for that. He had decided that she was an oddball with more money than intelligence; he supposed that she was running away from something, seeking some new but really non-existent Eden among the outer satellites. Very well. Let him continue to believe that, let him continue to think her a fool. He had no consideration for her personal feelings and with one brutal sentence he had robbed her of her dignity; with another he very nearly wiped out the funds in the Omaha bank. He had pretended not to want her charter and yet he was greedy for her money.

"Is there anything else?"

Webb raked her apparel with a critical glance. "You could trim down on the clothing—the less you wear the better. That bucket heats up."

"I beg your pardon?"

"Heat, sister, heat and discomfort. I haven't room for refrigerating gear and I wouldn't waste the money if there was room. Strip that stuff off or you'll regret it." He saw the sudden wary expression and laughed at the woman. "Oh, hell, cover it up if you want to hide it, but keep it thin —the lightweight stuff. Foil coveralls and a pair of magnetic shoes are all you need."

"What do you wear?" Kate asked faintly.

"Shorts." He exposed his arms and the burnt skin on his legs. "That crazy Singleton used to ride naked. The bucket gets hot."

"Singleton?"

"The dead one."

"Did he burn to death because of—what you said."

"He did not. He killed himself by stupidity. Hell, you won't burn much, not in just one trip. Something else: keep the luggage down to one suitcase; I can't afford weight. And that's about it. Get your papers checked, get some doctor to pass you for flight. I'll handle the rest of it when I take you through the field office." He gave her a sidelong glance. "Be prepared to spread some money around."

"What does that mean?"

"You haven't got clearance papers. You're going to have to buy some."

"Oh, yes, I understand."

"I thought you would. All right, get moving—you've got a lot to do. If we're lucky, we jump topside at midnight.

The name of my ship is the *Xanthus*. Be there two or three hours ahead of time."

"What a beautiful name, and a strange one. What does it mean?"

"My partner found it in a book," Webb explained. "Xanthus is a buried city or something like that. We use it because it's the only X in the registry. Easy to find and easy to remember."

"I approve of your partner's choice. It is a very lovely name." She hesitated and then asked, "The deceased partner? Mr. Singleton?"

"No—the one in jail. Singleton never read a book in his life; he used up all his intelligence committing suicide."

"Do you read much?"

"I like to read checks."

"Of course." The woman opened her purse and removed the checkbook. "I believe you said three thousand?"

"You know what I said."

Kate wrote out the check and handed it to Webb. He read it twice, smiled, and folded it away in a pocket. "Kate Bristol. I wondered if you had a name."

"I'm sorry, I forgot to introduce myself."

"*Miss* Bristol?"

"Yes."

"All right; be there about nine tonight. Check in at the purser's cage and put in a call for me. We'll clear away the red tape and get you on board." Webb strode away from the woman. Pausing on the doorstep, he glanced over his shoulder and was surprised to find her still there. "What are you waiting for?" he demanded dourly. "Get those papers squared away."

She snapped shut the purse and then played with the catch. "Mr. Webb, you said the . . . the convenience lacked a door. Would it be possible to place a door on it? After all, we will be together for several weeks—surely you can spare *that* much weight."

He laughed rudely, enjoying her flushed face. "Hell, yes, if you want one."

"Thank you." Kate left him then, walking with the slow measured tread cultivated by tall women to avoid awkwardness. The stately beat of the sharp heels moved around the house and died away in the late afternoon. Webb pulled the check from his pocket to read it once more. Statuesque woman, statuesque money. (And she'd damn well peel off those stifling clothes after a while and he'd get a look at the statuesque body.) The sum and the expectation afforded him a pleasing, buoyant sensation.

Webb waved the check toward the many holes dug into the turf behind the house. "Look, kid! And you don't get a penny of it. Your bad luck, boy—your stupid bad luck. Remember to watch the air pressure next time, if there is a next time." The check was again tucked away but Webb tarried, looking at the dozens of little graves.

Night was coming on, Singleton. Darkness. But then it had been dark down *there* for several hours, hadn't it? Dismally dark down there since the undertaker fastened the coffin lid and the gravedigger had shoveled dirt into the hole. You should have remembered to watch the pressure. Watch that air pressure, if you're flying buckets in hell now —and don't trust anyone else's handiwork. The first mistake is the last. You're grounded, Singleton.

Kate Bristol said, "So this is the bucket."

"This is the bucket," Webb acknowledged.

"It doesn't seem so small."

"You're not inside yet."

"Xanthus is a pretty name," she replied, "but some of the paint is peeling away."

Webb stared briefly at the camouflage on her face and then picked up the suitcase to climb away from her. After a moment of indecision the passenger abandoned her inspection of the ship's exterior and followed him up the ladder to the airlock, swinging with an easy grace. Webb noted that and remembered the blows on his mouth. He passed through the lock, followed a cramped passageway for a distance and then climbed another ladder. She stayed at his heels. The second climb terminated on a tiny landing. Webb shoved open the hatch beyond the landing and they were in the cabin.

"Surprise," he said sourly.

The cabin was nearly the shape of a truncated cone and about twelve feet wide at the base, its broadest dimension; from the hatchway it stretched forward some eighteen feet to end on a gently curving bulkhead. Above, it was twice the height of a man at the inner wall but again the ceiling sloped to meet the deck at starboard. Two narrow bunks hanging one above the other, and three lockers standing in normal fashion occupied the port wall near at hand. Be-

yond the lockers a minute galley was fitted into a wall recess, with storage water protruding from the wall directly
below it. Someone had pasted an oversize starmap on the
forward bulkhead.

The remainder of the inhospitable cabin was given over
to the apparatus necessary for operating the ship. The gear
was tightly packed into every cranny of the cabin—with
some of it hanging overhead—so as to suggest that the room
had never known a layout design, that everything was simply thrown in and bolted down when the vessel was otherwise completed. Kate studied the cramped cabin and finally
dropped her gaze to the aisle, a relatively unimpeded walking space down the center. She judged it to be six feet wide
and perhaps fifteen feet in length, providing one dodged
around a squat chunk of machinery occupying the exact
center of the cabin. Six by fifteen feet: home for the next
few weeks.

"What's that thing in the middle of the floor?"

"That thing in the middle of the *deck* is the auto pilot.
The plotting room charts our course on tape and I feed the
tape into the pilot. If nobody has made a mistake it gets
us there after a while."

"Everything is so small, so cramped."

"It's big enough for me," he said significantly.

Kate asked, "Are we leaving at midnight?"

"No, they're still loading cargo. The tower is saving me
a hole on the six o'clock booster. Six in the morning."
Webb offered a broad wink and rapped his knuckles on a
newly-hung sheet of fiberglass. "Look, I put a door on the
head."

"Thank you. And which is my bunk, please?"

"Topside."

She examined it with misgivings, acutely aware of where
that placed the man. "I trust these Van Allen bags are
spaceworthy. I don't want to burn."

"They'll do," Webb said. "We go through the belts in a
helluva hurry."

"What is your cargo, if I may ask?"

"Hardware—automated stuff, all kinds of robot mon-
keys." He pounded the bulkhead with heady exhilaration.
"I'm taking on an automaton down there big enough to
run a radio telescope. It *will* drive a radio telescope; there
is enough hardware to keep the thing running forever, I
guess. Priority hardware, every scrap of it. Those damned

bureaucrats stalled for eight or ten years and then made up their minds yesterday." He clasped his palms together in an avaricious gesture. "They're paying for the priority now—paying through the nose. Bureaucrats like it that way, sudden and expensive. I'll take their money."

Kate knew a pang of apprehension. "Where are we going?"

"The Tombaugh," he chortled triumphantly, "all the way out to the Tombaugh, and its costing those bureaucrats a sweet lot of money!"

She felt back, sharply dismayed.

There was no need to ask for further information on that destination. She knew. The Tombaugh Station was civilization's single outpost on Pluto, the smallest and furthermost speck of human habitation in the coldest reaches of the solar system. The Tombaugh was an observatory, the only one beyond Callisto, and it was the nearest neighbor to X. She remembered reading that a huge radio telescope was part of the Tombaugh's equipment, together with an astrograph, a twenty-four inch reflector, and a Schmidt camera for a program of comet observation. Only a handful of men lived there to maintain the watch.

Pluto was a cruel, inhospitable world; its four thousand mile diameter contained nothing other than a low, dense atmosphere of icy hydrogen and helium, closely hugging frozen methane seas which in turn were imbedded on a rocky core; a world largely unexplored and unmapped; raw, barren, mountainous and all but useless to man. Pluto was inutile and nearly untenable, so remote in space that the sun was but a brilliant, spectacular star. The most recent report she'd read said that at Pluto's perihelion, just past, surface illumination was equal to only three hundred times that of moonlight. The forbidding temperature of almost four hundred degrees below zero discouraged all activity except one: the operation of the observatory.

The Tombaugh was an excellent observatory for its lonely vigil, being perched on a mountainous crag well above the smothering atmosphere of Pluto.

It watched X, the tenth planet of the solar system.

X was the true Trans-Neptune, the planet Lowell had been seeking when he found Pluto. It was only ten years old by popular reckoning and swung in a vast, leisurely orbit more than one thousand million miles beyond Pluto. The skeptics professed to see no reason for ever visiting it.

X had an inappreciable albedo and an anticipated large size combined with a low density; it possessed a frigid and lethal atmosphere in keeping with the outer planets, and at least four satellites. Its outermost moon, circling the primary at more than three million miles, had been suggested as the next stepping stone to the stars.

Ten years ago a startled Brazilian radar operator aboard a patrol ship had found X and almost at once, to study it, the Tombaugh Station was erected on Pluto's jutting crags —the most advantageous window imaginable short of an actual landing on that outermost moon. X was the center of scientific discussion and of public fancy. The hottest question concerning it was that one debated in numerous intergovernmental conventions: should the Tombaugh be dismantled, now that it's immediate usefulness was coming to an end?

For Pluto was rapidly pulling away from X, dropping the new planet behind in remote darkness. For a period of about forty years Pluto was, in effect, the eighth planet from the sun, because its peculiar path brought it inside the orbit of Neptune, and by exerting the utmost effort, small freighters such as Webb's bucket could reach the eccentric wanderer. But now, in the summer months of 2009, Pluto was swiftly nearing the end of its visit; within a short time it would again cross Neptune's orbit for its long retreat outward.

Kate recalled the debated questions: should the Tombaugh be dismantled for salvage value? Or should it be abandoned, at least until Pluto's next return two and a half centuries hence? Or, and this was most tempting, should the station be outfitted for non-human operation, to maintain a robotic sweep of the heavens during its two hundred and forty-eight year orbit about the sun?

Webb's damned bureaucrats had acted at the last possible moment. The most tempting question had carried and they were loading on board a cargo of automatons.

"Look at that goddam thing!"

Kate was jerked from her reverie. She found him forward fussing over the radar, and two short steps brought her to his side. "What's the matter with it?"

"Look," he bellowed, "the damned thing's got a bug!"

She looked but saw only an erratic, jumbled shimmer washing over the screen. It reminded her of a slow, majestic tide sweeping across an empty beach.

"What kind of bug?"

Webb's reply was a shout. "If I knew that I could do something about it." He jerked the electric cord from its receptacle and began dismantling the unit. "It wasn't like this yesterday!" He pulled on something inside and then swore when his fingers slipped, skinning his knuckles. A moment later a transformer came free and was hurled across the deck. The replacement was accompanied by a rolling commentary which had little bearing on the matter.

"Don't mind me," Kate said. "I know all the words."

Webb ignored her and continued working. But when the new transformer failed to correct the trouble the flow of colorful words doubled, and he started pulling bits and parts elsewhere in the unit.

"Excuse me," Kate offered at last, "I only thought I knew them all. That remark about Titania and Oberon is new to me. But aren't they of the same sex?"

"Moons, not people," he replied witheringly.

She considered that. "I still don't understand it."

When Webb had done everything he could think of, the erratic tide continued to wash across the radar screen. "I wish Jimmy Cross was here," he said in utter disgust. "This is his meat."

"Who is Jimmy Cross?"

"The one in jail."

"Ah, the other partner. And he is a mechanic?"

Webb ignored the question and moved along the narrow aisle to his miniature teletype. He opened the machine.

XANTHUS TO TORCON: I HAVE A RADAR GHOST. WHOSE FAULT? X

"What is Torcon?" Kate wanted to know.

"The tower across the field—Toronto Control."

"And X indicates the end of the message?"

"Yes." A bell sounded and a moment later the teletype delivered his answer.

TORCON TO XANTHUS: GHOST IS EVERY-WHERE. YOUR FAULT. X

"Thanks," Webb said sarcastically to the distant teletype operator. "Now why don't you come down here and fix it?"

Wearily, he opened a locker to remove a bag of tools. The bag was flung into the aisle and Webb began dismantling the radar unit a second time, resigned to a long task.

Kate Bristol watched him for a while and then, tired of the continual flow of profanity, she climbed into the upper bunk and wriggled into her Van Allen bag. She tried to shut the sound of his voice out of her ears.

She was rudely awakened some hours later when he smacked the underside of the bunk with a heavy fist, jolting her into awareness. There were heavy sounds somewhere in the bowels of the ship and after a moment it seemed to swing like a pendulum. Webb scampered about the cabin, slamming and bolting hatches and retrieving useless tools. She watched him run into the toilet cubicle to make sure the drain locks were closed and then he slammed the door —the new door. The pressure pumps were started and they made a maddening racket within the confines of the tiny cabin. He opened the teletype and the radar, and cursed again. She realized the bug hadn't been removed.

Webb made a final inspection of the cabin and its appointments and slid into the lower bunk. "Strap in," he shouted as he dug a hard finger into her rump, "We're jumping topside."

"Stop poking me! I am strapped in—after all, I'm no novice." But she was also inside the Van Allen bag, forgetting that it wasn't needed as yet. "How high will the booster carry us?"

"About twenty miles, and then throw us away."

Twenty miles. According to those reports, Singleton had lost his life about twenty miles up and the twin vacuum locks had been responsible. Kate asked, "Will we go into orbit?"

"Everybody goes into orbit," Webb replied. "You ain't a green hand, eh? The booster throws us into a plotted orbit, but we're on our own when we climb toward apogee the second time. We hightail it for Titan."

"Is it always so noisy?"

"You'll get used to that. Live with it for a week and you can hear me whisper." He stopped to listen. She detected no change in the general noise level but he seemed to hear something below. "Here it comes!"

The brutal surge smashed into her stomach and robbed her of wind; queer, annoying fingers of creeping darkness probed her mind. She tried to push them away but failed. The *Xanthus* rode skyward on the booster rocket.

The cabin was measurably quieter.

Irvin Webb sprawled on the deck with his back to the sloping starboard hull and watched the young woman in the radiation sack recover consciousness. The noisy booster which had thrown them into orbit was long gone, dropping earthward, and the cabin seemed relatively peaceful. Webb was amused at his passenger.

She fidgeted uncomfortably in the bag, stretched out her long legs to ease the cramp and then cautiously put her hands through the opening at the top. A moment later the folds of the sack were pulled away and her cosmetic-laden face appeared. The face peered around the cabin in brief bewilderment and then discovered Webb on the deck. He was wearing nothing more than faded khaki shorts and magnetic shoes. She noted that he hadn't shaved.

"What are you doing out of bed?" she demanded.

"What are you doing in the sack?" he countered. "My engines haven't fired yet. We're in orbit."

"Oh, of course. Where in orbit?"

"Approaching perigee. We'll pass and climb in a little while. You might as well stay there."

"I've never fainted before," she said to herself.

"You've never jumped topside in a bucket before. This isn't the deluxe tour, Bristol, and this ain't no stinking ferryboat. I can't waste time nor money on the featherbed treatment." He waved toward the star map on the forward bulkhead. "The Tombaugh is better than nine weeks away. I expect to get there before it makes ten."

"Nine weeks!" she repeated incredulously.

"One thousand, five hundred and eighty-four hours port-to-port. A shade better than nine weeks, I guess. But cheer up, Bristol, we've already spent an hour or so. See how fast it goes?"

"I'm not frightened, Mr. Webb. I haven't said anything about quitting."

"No, you haven't," Webb agreed, "But you *are*. I'm dumping you on Titan."

She struggled against the straps. "You are what?"

"Titan is the end of the line for you—charter ended. Titan is my refueling point; I have to lay over a few hours and convert to methane for the big jump. I'll help you down with your suitcase."

"You'll do no such thing!"

He shrugged. "Then carry it yourself."

"That isn't what I meant! I will *not* disembark on Titan. I chartered for the duration."

"Wait and see," he promised. "Titan is the end."

"But why?" she demanded. "Why?"

Webb asked roughly, "What the hell can *you* do on the Tombaugh, Bristol? Take dictation? Play hostess? Polish the dominoes? Bull. Those jokers will be working their fool heads off setting up this new hardware before Pluto runs away with them—did you ever know a star-peep to waste time with a woman when he can play with a telescope?" He was scoffing. "What good will you be out there?"

"I won't be in the way. I will stay on board and come back with this ship, with you."

"This bucket ain't coming back," Webb said.

"You are coming home without your ship?"

"Without," Webb repeated and smote the deck beneath him. "Last trip for this old bucket. Well done, gung ho and all that bilge. There's no refueling depot on Pluto, I can't bring her back." He rubbed his unshaven chin. "If the government had made this decision a couple of years ago it would have been different. I could have managed the round trip after refueling on Titan—I could have taken my time and coasted both ways. But not now, not this trip. Time is too short and the Tombaugh is outward bound. It's running away from me at three miles per second. The only thing to do now is run like hell, set down on the Tombaugh and abandon ship. The old bucket won't rust."

"Will you simply walk away and leave it?"

"I'll walk away and leave it. Done—finished. I'm getting my money out of it, the damned bureaucrats are covering the loss. And that's why you aren't going out there—I can't bring you back."

"But how will you get back?"

"The government has a cruiser standing by. We unload the bucket, help the star-peeps set up their new gear, and then jump for home. We give Pluto back to the icicles or whatever—the robots run the station after that. And you disembark when I reach refueling orbit over Titan."

"I think it's unfair," Kate protested.

"They can't use speedy typists on the Tombaugh, and you wouldn't volunteer for other things."

"Don't be vulgar!"

Webb got up from the deck to don his suit and check the chronometer. "It's coming up fast now."

"What is your perigee?"

"Twenty-three miles. We just passed it. Singleton got it about here."

A strident clamor from the bowels of the auto pilot echoed his words and cut off her following question. Webb leaped into his bunk and burrowed into the depths of his Van Allen bag. He found himself looking at the curvy underside of the bunk above. "Now, Bristol," he shouted. "Pull that bag over your head when my engines fire."

"What is happening?"

"We're climbing away from perigee and the tapes are taking over—they've moved the hot brick into the furnace and the fuel is heating up. Stay in that bag until I give you the high sign—don't forget there are two zones up there."

"I remember."

The engines fired. They were felt before they were heard, although the two sensations were so close as to be one. There was no impression of the ship leaping forward or climbing or any other sense of motion. Their bodies sagged gently toward the vessel's stern and a moment later their stomachs and eviscera attempted to follow. The sound of the atomic engines permeated the tiny cabin.

Kate ducked into the safety of the leaded cloth bag. . . .

The woman wriggled free of the confining folds of the Van Allen bag and climbed to the deck. Once there she found it necessary to brace her feet and keep a steadying hand on the bunk railing to maintain equilibrium. The cabin was unusually warm and after a cautionary hesitation she removed the airsuit. She was clad in cream colored coveralls.

Webb was forward, scowling at the radar screen. He had already stripped down to the khaki shorts, revealing his blackened, over-exposed skin. Cancer scars like tiny craters marred the visible parts of his body.

"Mr. Webb," she said severely, "I warned you once. There will be no second warning."

His only response was a crooked grin as he swept the lines of the creamy coveralls.

"I don't like being poked, punched or mauled," she continued. "You can tell me what you have to say."

Webb said, "Sure," and turned his attention to the teletype. His slow message was punched on two fingers.

XANTHUS TO TORCON: ALL CLEAR. GHOST
CONTINUES HERE. QUERY. X.

The reply came after a short interval. Webb read it and cursed the Toronto operator for his barely concealed levity. Kate read the reply over his shoulder.

TORCON TO XANTHUS: GHOST DEPARTED
WITH YOU. LOCAL SCREENS CLEAR NOW.
PACIFY YOUR POLTERGEIST.

"What the hell is a poltergeist?" Webb growled.

Kate shook her head. "Please don't ask me." Turning to scan the radar, she found pips moving over the screen. "What are those?"

"A couple more buckets—they came up on the booster with us. One is the *Yandro* and the other is the *Skyhook III*. We're all running for the Tombaugh." He looked at the screen with disgust. "What's wrong? What's leaking?"

"I'm sure I don't know."

"Jimmy Cross would fix it in a hurry." And then, surprisingly, he answered a question she had asked quite some time ago. "Yeah, he's a mechanic. And a good one. He could fix or un-fix anything with his eyes shut."

"And Mr. Singleton?"

"What about Singleton? He was a punk kid."

"While we were still in orbit, you said that Singleton got it 'just about here.' You've dropped several hints about the man but you've told me nothing about him. Mr. Webb, what about Singleton? Either tell me what happened to him, or don't mention his name again."

Webb eyed her dourly and grunted. "Come here." He led the way to the toilet cubicle and flung the door open. "See those two levers mounted on the wall? You push one and *then* you push the other. One at a time. It's an airlock and it dumps the waste matter. Simple, eh?"

"Primitive, but simple," she agreed.

"Sure." Webb slammed the door shut, venting his annoyance on the thing. "There's always an hour or two in orbit; a man can knock around and take care of the little things while he's waiting. Singleton got the bright idea that he wanted to use the head. Of all times, he waits until he reaches orbit and then wants to use the head. So he used it. And then the damned fool flushed away his air pressure. He was dead in fifty or a hundred seconds."

"But couldn't someone have—"

"He was alone," Webb cut her off. "He was taking a load to the Arzachel Crater and he was so damned dumb he couldn't get to the moon without killing himself. The kid was naked, he liked to ride that way, and he was passing time before the Van Allen belts. So he boiled to death in his own juice—blood, saliva, tears, everything boiled."

Kate said faintly, "Your ship should be equipped with safety devices."

"It is," Webb retorted. "Use one hand and press one lever at a time. You can't beat common sense as a safety device. Don't lay on both of them with the length of your arm—that's no way to handle airlock valves."

"But why was the other partner jailed?"

"Suspicion of murder. Jimmy Cross had just overhauled several pieces of gear before the kid took off for the moon, and the cops figure Jimmy did something to foul the kid." Webb rubbed the stubble of beard. "The insurance company must think so too—they haven't paid off yet."

"*Is* it possible for a mechanic to jam the device?"

"A good mechanic can fix or foul anything," Webb said savagely. "The cops dug around in the bulkheads, looking for wires or something to prove that the two valves were rigged to open together—for all the good it did them. Singleton killed himself and that was that!"

The drive motors cut off abruptly.

Kate reached out a quick hand to steady herself and then braced her feet apart on the deck. "What's the matter?" she asked in alarm.

"Nothing. We're coasting—it's programmed on the tapes. You was as well get used to it, we'll be doing it off and on all the way." He grinned at her discomfiture. "You can't drive an old bucket like this at speed *all* the time—it might fall apart."

She nodded and sat down on the deck, hugging her boots to hold herself there. She wondered at the mild surprise she had read on his face when the motors stopped.

The old ship bored outward for endless hours and a pattern of life within the cramped confines of the cabin gradually asserted itself. They ate, slept, paced the narrow aisle, sat on it, lay on it, and picked or nagged at threads of conversation. She was plainly bored with the journey but Webb seemed to enjoy the solitude. The *Xanthus* drove for Titan in fitful spurts, destroying time and distance.

Less than a hundred hours from their destination a floater intercepted them.

Webb was awakened in his bunk by Bristol shaking his shoulder. He pushed her off and rolled over to listen to his ship; it was a motion performed by habit each time he regained consciousness, a brief moment of total vigilance during which his senses tested the sound and feel of the vessel for rightness.

She said, "There are several messages on the teletype you should read, something about a floater. What is a floater?"

"A derelict," Webb grunted and placed the palm of his hand on the bulkhead to listen to the vibrations. "Let the damned thing float—I've got a schedule to keep."

"I think you had better read these, Mr. Webb. And you should look at your radar screen."

He was out of the bunk before she finished, staring at the blip on the screen. "Where did *that* come from?"

"It has been there for several hours."

"Why in the hell didn't you wake me?" he barked. "The damned thing is too close—it might skin me."

"I thought it was that ship you mentioned earlier, the *Yandro*. Aren't they all coming in on Titan to refuel?"

"They won't come that close! Jehosaphat—it's going to skin me for sure." Webb whirled to the auto pilot and stopped the tapes. The bucket was now dropping tail-first toward Titan and he took over manual control to increase deceleration. After several minutes he cut the engines and glanced again at the radar.

"What did the teletype say? Read the last one."

"*Torcon to Xanthus*," she read aloud, "*Alert. Floater off tape Amarcon to Titan. Clamoring. Approximate locus BG 90037YY crossed BA 34345YY. Ownership reward posted Amarcon advise if. X.*"

"I can't understand any part of it," Kate commented.

Webb jotted down the figures and then compared them to his own. "Skinned!" he yelled at her, and again applied decelerating force. While the motors were still firing he turned attention to his steering rockets and loosed jets of pressurized gas, altering course a fraction of a degree. She could see no change in position of the blip on the screen but Webb seemed satisfied for the moment.

"What is Amarcon?" Kate asked. "Which tower is that?"

"Amarillo, Texas, Amarillo launched that ship."

"But what happened to it?"

"How the devil would I know? Anything could have happened—maybe it met a rock, there are rocks as big as houses out here." He pulled the typed message from her fingers, studying it. "It's wrecked, because the distress signal is clamoring. Off tape means that the impact, or whatever it was, damaged the auto pilot or ruined his tapes. He's falling free in whatever direction he was kicked."

"What is the meaning of that last line?"

"The owners have posted a recovery bond at Amarillo. Torcon wants to know if I'm going after it."

"Are you?"

Webb eyed the blip carefully. "I might. I just might. I've lost tape now anyway—I'll have to take it into refueling orbit on manual." He swung around to grin at the woman. "I could use the money."

"Of course. I imagine that you are penniless."

The teletypewriter came to excited life to underscore her words. Webb flicked a meaningful finger and she pulled out the sheet to read it.

"Torcon to Xanthus; Emergency repeat emergency. Derelict riding your collision course 46 hours plus minus 12 minutes. Take evasive action. Advise. X."

Webb rammed his hands into his pockets and laughed. "Hell, yes, I'm going after him! You can tell 'em that."

Webb found the silhouette looming before him and threw out his legs to land gently feet-first on the hull, knowing that the noise of his arrival could be heard by anyone within the ship—if it still contained air and if anyone was alive to listen. The derelict vessel was small and slimly rounded and he thought he recognized the type: a fast, sporty job, outshopped at Toledo at premium prices for people who thought they could afford such jellyboats. Moving carefully, he crawled around the hull and was surprised to find the airlock open. A blinking light in the lock was the only thing to meet his startled gaze.

He slid in, closed the outer valve and punched for entry. The ship's interior opened to him and he found a wide and

wasteful corridor serving three rooms. Webb was astonished at the opulent waste—three rooms and a corridor
under pressure! A quick glance forward revealed that the
third and last room was the pilot's hutch, but nearer at
hand were two open doors giving glimpses of private cab-
ins. Webb stepped into the corridor. The first cabin to fall
under his scrutiny was empty and he passed it by, noting
only that it contained a low bed—not a bunk.

In the second cabin the suited figure of a man lay supine
on clean sheets. The man was alive and lifted a hand to
wave a weak greeting. Webb returned the greeting and then
stepped closer.

The survivor was handcuffed. His other hand was manacled to a small black box and the box was again cuffed
to the stanchion supporting the bed.

"I'll be damned!" Webb said aloud. "You a crook?"

"Courier," was the whispered answer. "The pilot has the
key."

"I think the pilot stepped outside a long ways back,"
Webb said brutally. He looked around the expensive cabin.
The fellow stayed in bed because he was securely fastened
to it; he could not reach the galley built into the opposite
wall, nor the doorway, nor anyplace that was more than a
foot or two distant from the stanchion. "How long have you
been there?"

"I don't know," was the tired whisper. "Lost count."

"What's in the black box—must be pretty hot stuff?"

"Don't know," the courier repeated. "I wasn't told."

"Hell of a note," Webb said. "I'll look for a hacksaw or
something."

He quit the cabin and went forward to the pilot's cubicle. The place was minute—actually cramped—but it contained everything a man would need or desire to move his
ship between planets. In that first sweeping glance Webb
knew an overpowering envy of that cockpit—it was the
kind of a cockpit (and the kind of a ship) that he would
never be able to afford, no matter how much money the
damned bureaucrats dumped into his lap.

The radar was still operating and he saw his own bucket
on the screen. A key hung above the radar, and Webb
pulled it from its fastener in frowning wonder. There was
no ignition lock on the control board to receive that key,
and he found himself looking back down the corridor with
puzzled concentration. The noise of the teletype brought

him around. It was a wonderfully compact model, fitted into a recess in the bulkhead.

> XANTHUS TO TORCON: WEBB ENROUTE TO DERELICT, WILL CLAIM BOND. PAYING PASSENGER ORDERED TO DISEMBARK TITAN, DESPITE HER PROTESTS. UNHAPPY. X

"The hell you are!" he roared in anger. "Now, the *hell* you are. Ain't that too goddam bad?" He ripped the message from the machine and tucked it into a flap pocket.

After a moment he remembered his mission and searched for the auto pilot. It was artfully concealed behind a sliding panel in the bulkhead, and a soft sticky plastic scattered over the base of the robot provided a clue to the riddle of the ship. The tapes were broken, of course, and with their parting the motors had stopped, setting off the distress signal. Webb traced a gloved finged through the fallen plastic and guessed how death had come to the sleek vessel. A hurtling rock or other bit of deadly something had pierced the hull at precisely the wrong spot, smashing through the twin hulls and the inner layer of insulating plastic to strike the auto pilot. Toledo couldn't have prevented that.

Webb checked the pressure gauge and found it normal. After the piercing, then, the pilot had gone topside to repair the puncture, allowing the pressure to rebuild itself. The man's next move should have been to call his tower and reassure them, but this man hadn't returned from his patching chore; he was still out there somewhere in the darkness—the open airlock told that, and the drifting of the ship and the hungry, manacled courier underscored it. The damned fool had gone topside and tumbled off—or was knocked off. Too bad for him. The first mistake is the last and that pilot evidently committed it.

Webb made an entry in the vessel's log to protect his recovery claim and quit the throne room.

The waiting courier revealed his surprise when Webb unlocked the cuffs. "Where did you get the key?"

"Top secret—security regulations, and all that bilge. What do you suppose is in that damned box?" Webb pulled the courier to his feet. "Let's get going." But he was dissatisfied with the courier's slow progress and pulled his feet free of the deck to tow him.

They stopped in the airlock and Webb turned his head to look back. The first nagging doubt struck him there.

It was no more than a small jabbing suspicion but he couldn't shake it off. Planting the courier, he moved back into the brilliantly lighted corridor and stared the empty length of it. The derelict seemed filled with his quick mistrust. Webb prowled cautiously along the corridor, retracing his earlier route of exploration. Every detail fell beneath his doubting scrutiny. The first cabin with its door hanging awry (the cabin and the bed had been used), the next cabin and its door (of course it had been used, with immaculate sheets on both beds), the remaining cuffs still fastened to the stanchion, the tiny cockpit (complete to the last beautiful appointment). There seemed to be nothing amiss.

But something was.

Webb looked at the radar screen, at the pressure gauge, at the fuel indicators, at the clip that had held the key, at the broken tapes, at the scattered bits of plastic, at the teletype, at the star compass. What could be found wrong with all that? The vessel was in tidy order in those places where order was expected; it was in proper disorder in those places where disorder must be. Why then, should he be pricked with uncertainty? Why should he mistrust the derelict?

The haunting doubt remained.

In foul temper, Webb buckled the survivor to his belt and jumped for the *Xanthus*.

Kate Bristol's eyes widened when she saw the courier but Webb missed that and the glances exchanged between them. He buckled the man into the lower bunk and said, "Feed him." And then he went forward to the teletypewriter.

XANTHUS TO PROMISED LAND TITAN: APPROACHING YOU NINE HOURS LATE, SHALL KEEP ASSIGNED ORBIT OR WILL YOU SUBSTITUTE? REQUIRE RE-PLOT, ORBIT TO TOMBAUGH, MUST CLEAR FAST. TWO PASSENGERS DISEMBARKING TITAN: ONE MONEY & TICKET GUESTHOUSE, ONE HOSPITAL AMARCON SPONSORSHIP. X

Not waiting for the reply, Webb dropped tools in his pocket and went below decks to begin the job of converting his engines to methane. The hatch slammed behind him.

Kate pushed herself toward the hatch and listened. When she was certain that Webb was really gone, she sped back to the courier in the bunk. The man was already twisting and squirming in his suit, seeking to reach something concealed inside. In a moment he brought out a tiny key and unlocked the box shackled to his wrist.

"Take this quickly," the courier urged. "Give me your radio. Hurry, before he returns."

"You are the last man I expected to see out here," Kate exclaimed, still surprised at his appearance.

"Never mind that! Give me your radio—quickly!"

"But what are *you* doing here?"

"For heaven's sake, Kate, I'm bringing you a new radio. *Take it.* Yours is defective—hadn't you noticed?" And he pressed into her hand the counterpart to that emergency instrument given her by the communications office of the insurance company. "You're fouling every screen within thousands of miles—hundreds of thousands of miles."

"The ghost!" Kate exclaimed.

"Yes. The boys in Communications realized the error as soon as this ship left Toronto; the interference vanished with your departure. *Give me your radio!*"

She whirled away to vanish behind the newly hung door. The courier watched the closed hatch fearfully, expecting Webb to return before she did. After some moments the woman was back and the courier snatched the defective radio from her grasp, to lock it away in the little black box.

"The radio will be dismantled after I land," he said. "I don't dare touch it now, lest he become suspicious."

"But the derelict, the floater—"

"My ship is not now and never was a derelict. The pilot is still on board and he will continue to drift with the vessel until it is intercepted by the patrol, or until you are safely out of range. He concealed himself below deck. The piece was cut from whole cloth to trap Webb—our people gambled on Webb's greed."

"But it seemed such a genuine collision."

"It *would* have been a genuine collision if Webb had not avoided it; the authenticity was necessary, don't you see? Webb would avoid it, of course, and we knew he would also inspect the floater if it meant additional money to him."

"But what would have happened if Webb simply dodged around you and went on his way?"

"We would have continued floating. But another man

with another radio would have met you in orbit over Titan."

"Another one!"

"Certainly. The supervisor was overlooking nothing."

"Too bad," Kate said, "Webb is booting me off the ship at Titan. He's cancelling my charter."

"I doubt that," the courier replied. "The man who will meet you in orbit is an attorney. One of our people. Tell him your troubles if you wish to stay aboard."

The teletypewriter said:

PROMISED LAND TITAN TO XANTHUS: MAINTAIN ASSIGNED ORBIT, SAME NOW OPEN TO YOU. RE-PLOT READY SOON. LAUNCH MEET YOU IN ORBIT TO REMOVE TWO PASSENGERS. WELCOME LADY. X

"A measure of fame, I suppose," Kate commented.

When Webb returned to the cabin she was spooning hot soup into the courier. The man seemed to eat it greedily. Some of the soup spilled down onto his beard.

The government launch *Kteic* approached Webb's ship, matched speeds and locked on. When the crew had secured the transfer tube from airlock to airlock, Kate Bristol and the courier were moved to the launch. Webb did not hide his relief at their going.

"I want to thank you, sir," the courier said in parting. "Taking me off the derelict means more than you know, and I am properly grateful."

Webb waved him off. "Never mind that bilge. Just make sure that joker in Amarillo sends me my money."

"I find that touching, Mr. Webb," Kate intervened. "So much in character. As for myself, I am looking forward to a bath. I have endured more than three hundred and fifty hours on this—this tub, and I need a bath."

"Get the hell off my ship!" Webb roared.

Within minutes after the launch had pulled away another gentle bump sounded on the hull as the methane tanker locked on topside, to begin refueling operations. Webb snatched up a pair of methane nozzles from the tool locker and sped aft to the engine room to complete the change-over. Not until he was finished did he realize that he hadn't thoroughly inspected that derelict after all—he hadn't gone below for a look at its power plant.

The two ships orbited together for nearly three hours, making the bucket ready for the long jump.

Minutes before departure the launch returned with the new tapes, alloting him one thousand, two hundred and twenty-six hours to reach Tombaugh. Webb snatched the tapes and fitted them into his auto pilot, completing the job and turning to begin some other task before he realized that the launch had also brought him two newcomers. They stood just inside the hatch, looking at him.

Webb exploded with rage. "I told you to get the hell off my ship!" he yelled at Kate Bristol. And to the man beside her, "Who are you? What the hell you doing here?"

"My name is Abraham Calkins, sir. May we come aboard?" He flourished a calling card and handed it to Webb.

"You are aboard—now get off!" Webb read the card. "A jackleg, a damned jackleg!"

A shadow passed over Calkins' face but his voice remained smooth. "A brief moment, sir, and I shall be on my way. I realize you are facing a deadline of some few minutes, but I represent Miss Bristol in this matter."

"I'm hauling out of here when those tapes fire," Webb retorted. "I've got to catch the Tombaugh—I'm not going to go chasing a dirty ball of ice along the rim of the solar system," He blinked. "What matter?"

"Miss Bristol's passage, sir. The matter of the original charter."

"What the hell are you talking about?"

"I shall make it clear. Miss Bristol chartered this vessel at Toronto for a sum of money agreed upon in advance. The sum was paid and her acceptance is now a matter of record. It was her desire to engage transportation to one of the Outer Moons, and you agreed to lend your vessel for that purpose. You reserved the right to select the ultimate destination, subject to cargo demands, and she agreed to the reservation. All this is correct, is it not?"

"Keep talking—fast."

"Very well. Now then, in due course you took on cargo which was consigned to the Tombaugh Station, on Pluto. Miss Bristol did not cancel the charter upon learning that information, nor did you. There was no refund of monies. Therefore the verbal contract between you, augmented by the written records on file at Toronto, remained in effect when you left that port. The contract is still binding, sir. The lady still retains charter on this vessel."

"Bully! Are we *all* going to the Tombaugh? This bucket is jumping orbit pretty damned quick."

"I am sorry, sir, but your vessel will not leave orbit without fulfilling the contract." He displayed a legal form in blue binding. "I have here a writ of legal attachment on this vessel. A law enforcement officer is waiting in the launch. Unless I release you, the writ will be served and the launch will stand by to make sure you remain in orbit."

"Damn you, you can't hold me here!"

"I can and will, sir, with the assistance of the officer and the launch." The attorney shrugged. "But you have your legal rights, of course. You are free to contest our claim in the courts. You may return to the Promised Land with us now, if you wish, and I am sure the case can be heard within two or three days."

"I can't wait two or three days," Webb bellowed. "I'm jumping in two or three minutes! *Get clear.*"

"No, sir."

"Damn you, I'm going to Pluto. I only agreed to take her to one of the moons."

Calkins smiled in satisfaction as if he had been waiting for that. "Mr. Webb, surely you know that Pluto is a satellite, an escaped satellite. It is not impossible that a court of law might define it as an "outer moon" within the context of the contract. It *has* been clearly established that Pluto was once a satellite of Neptune. Well, Mr. Webb?"

Webb fumed. He whirled to read the chronometer and realized that time was running out. "I've got government cargo for the Tombaugh. They want it delivered!"

"Yes, sir, you have exactly that. And I daresay, you did not see fit, to notify your government agency that you had already accepted a charter, prior to accepting their cargo. Nor did you cancel the agreement with my client after you accepted the cargo." The attorney smirked. "I believe a conflict of interest exists there, and it may prove an interesting point in the courts. And another several days, of course."

"I can't wait several days." Webb was sweating. "If I don't jump this damned orbit in the next minute or so I'll lose the Tombaugh. I can't chase it around the sun!"

"Precisely. And so we agree?"

"Dammit, she hasn't any business out there."

"That is not for you or me to say."

An ominous warning sounded in the bowels of the auto pilot and Webb whirled in desperation to punch the safety switch. "Move!" he snapped at the jackleg. "It's ready to fire."

"My client, sir?"

"Your client can rot in space for all I care. Move!"

"Are you agreeing to complete the charter, sir?"

"I don't care what she does—you get off the ship."

"Yes, sir. Thank you, sir." The attorney turned quickly to shake Bristol's hand. "May I wish you a pleasant voyage?" he jumped for the hatch and the ladder beyond. "This has been most rewarding, sir."

"*Get out!*" Webb watched the chronometer and counted the seconds. "Hurry, damn you, run!" he shouted after the fleeting man. A moment later the airlock closed and the transfer tube was broken. Webb groaned. "*Fifty seconds late.*" He lifted his hand from the safety switch and methane exploded from the nozzles, tearing the *Xanthus* from orbit. Webb was holding onto the auto pilot for support, knowing what was to come, but the sudden thrust hurled his passenger against the after bulkhead.

He refused to speak to her for more than three hundred hours.

"I have a lovely bath at the guesthouse," Kate said when the silence became unbearable. "Do I smell nice?"

Webb sulked and made doodles in his log. . . .

And later, "I forgot to take my suitcase with me when I quit the ship. Had you noticed that?"

Webb squatted by the galley fixing himself a meal. . . .

Much later, "It isn't as warm as it was at first. Is that because we are so far away from the sun?"

Webb read old messages on the teletypewriter. . . .

After uncounted hours, "You don't have to like it, Mr. Webb, but at least we can be civilized."

Webb lay in his bunk, studying the curved underside of the bunk above him. She was in it and causing the curve. He reached out a finger and let the nail trace an imaginary line along the posterior silhouette. . . .

After interminable days—or weeks—she asked, "Will it be possible to see the new planet on the radar?"

That one caused a spark. Webb glanced up from the unit and said, "The screen is clear now."

"Well," she exclaimed, "welcome back to the land of the living! I suppose the ghost got tired and just went away."

"Troubles don't just go away," Webb retorted moodily.

"Tell me, will it be possible to catch a glimpse of *X?* A new planet is a fascinating thing, isn't it? Will we see it on the radar?"

"Maybe, if the wind is right."

"What wind?"

"Oh—the wind. I've seen it a couple of times."

"Really? What was it like?"

"Fascinating," he said shortly.

"Now, please, let's not quarrel. Tell me about the Tombaugh Station. What is *it* like?"

Webb allowed his wandering gaze to drift along the topographical contours of her body. The tight clothing irked him. "Rocks, ice, methane. The same old stuff. Downright dismal place—the seas are frozen methane with little rocky islands sticking up through them. Frozen gas hanging on the rocks that looks like snow."

"But what about the observatory?"

"Well, it's a building," Webb said carelessly. "A little building hanging on the side of a mountain. Inside is the star-peeps' gear—telescopes and stuff. Downstairs are the living quarters and the communications rig. And outside, nearby, is the radio telescope. And beyond *that* is a plateau we use for a landing field."

"It doesn't sound very impressive as you tell it."

"Pimple on a mountainside," Webb grunted. "A frozen pimple on a frozen mountainside, with a bunch of half-frozen guys inside sitting around taking pictures. The Tombaugh ain't much, and Pluto is less than that."

"Have you seen the new planet in their telescope?"

"Those jokers won't allow that. You've got to have a union card or be from Cambridge."

"What do the astronomers do there?"

"Work. And sit."

"I mean when they aren't working?"

"I can't say—I never stayed around to watch them," Webb answered testily. "I set out my cargo and run."

"But isn't it frustrating to be so near *X* and not be allowed to look at it?"

"Nope. I haven't lost anything out yonder." He turned to the star map on the forward bulkhead and looked at the are representing the orbit of *X*. Someone had added a marginal notation: *mean 51 A.U.* "The thing will be making its perihelion passage in another hundred years or so, and somebody will try for it. It will be one hell of a long jump but some hero will try it. The system is crawling with witless heroes."

She offered some remark to keep the conversation going but Webb was already lost, sinking into introspection. His attention was drawn to the now faultlessly operating radar. What would Jimmy Cross have made of *that?*

When the bucket reached the half mark—six hundred and thirteen hours after jumping Titan's orbit—Webb was immersed in paper work. Using blank pages from the now almost useless log book, he was busily engaged in toting up the profits of the voyage beginning with the money Bristol had paid for passage and ending with the reward someone in Amarillo would pay for recovering the courier and his little black box. Webb didn't know exactly how much the reward would be, but in his mind he caused it to be a generous figure and accordingly added a generous figure into the column. On the debit side he deducted the costs of tapes, fuel, provisions, and the renting of the hot brick from the AEC. He liked profits. The end sum was a happy amount. (And still unaccounted for was the pay-off from Singleton's insurance, plus money from the sale of the house.)

Nice. Very nice. Let the bucket rot on Pluto. All this amounted to break-off money. He could quit.

A hundred hours later he was again dwelling on the damnable puzzle of the derelict. Webb was able to recreate sharp mental images of every corner of that sleek ship, and now he probed the images for faults. There *was* a fault there, somewhere. The conviction was too strong to ignore.

And sixty hours after that he was watching Bristol moping about the cabin, and wondering what lay beneath the skin-tight cream-colored coveralls. What was she hiding?

And a hundred and fifteen hours after that Webb again cursed the auto pilot because the tapes and the engines paused for the briefest moment—they were decelerating— and then went into action with nothing more than a strangled gasp of sound meant to be the prior warnings. The bucket was overdue for the junkpile. (And he found the woman watching him narrowly. Now, why?)

Some eighty hours later Webb pulled and scratched at

his itching beard and dozed over the radar. He was impatient for Pluto to show itself.

The courier had worn a beard.

Webb blinked and sat up.

The courier had worn a beard. Once more he pawed through the mental images of that derelict because it would not let him rest, would not permit peace of mind. In his imagination he turned over and examined again each item as he had first seen it, turned over every rock and stared at the thing which crawled away. The open lock, the blinking light, the first cabin and then the next, the soft beds, the manacled courier and his beard, the pilot's hutch, the broken tapes, the key, the fallen plastic, the radar, the teletypewriter—Bristol had sent a message from the *Xanthus* while he was visiting the derelict. And he had booted her off ship while orbiting Titan, but she had bounced right back with that damned jackleg. And somewhere along there his radar unit had rid itself of the ghost.

The whole of it was absurd.

Webb closed his eyes, the better to picture in vivid detail that courier's cabin. And the pilot's cubicle.

He worried those two images for fifteen or twenty minutes of frowning study, until at last his exclamation broke the silence of the cabin.

"Well, I'll be damned!"

The floater had revealed two flaws, not one.

Those tapes had been broken—or cut—while the auto pilot was at rest *not* while they were in motion and driving the engines. They had stopped in an unnatural manner. *If* the piercing had snapped them in mid-flight those two upper reels would have continued to turn under their own momentum, would have spilled loose tape down onto the base of the mechanism or out onto the deck. But he hadn't found them that way. He had discovered the tapes still neatly coiled on their upper reels, tightly wound. They had been stopped first—and then cut, or broken. The derelict was a fraud.

And the courier had overlooked a tidy detail to his story. His beard was the proper length but the chains to the manacles were not—they did not permit the man to reach the galley, or the doorway, or the toilet. Yet his sheets were clean and his clothing immaculate. (And the missing pilot had probably *not* gone overboard—he was probably hiding somewhere below decks, perhaps in that never inspected engine room.)

The derelict was a fraud, the pilot was in hiding and the courier had been a feeble liar. Webb roundly cursed himself for a stupid fool.

Kate said lazily, "And then the second pirate spat out a foul oath. I seem to be getting used to it."

Webb shot down the length of the aisle, rummaged in his locker and found the teletype message Kate had sent.

"Still unhappy?" he asked sarcastically, and dangled the paper in her face.

She read the danger signs and sat upright in her bunk, bracing her back against wall. "You told me to advise Torcon you were investigating the floater."

"I didn't tell you to add this bilge. But it worked, didn't it? That jackleg met the launch and figured out a way to keep you on board—you want to play tourist, you want to see Pluto."

"This may be my only opportunity," she answered mildly. "We will all be dead when the planet comes around again."

"Some of us might be dead this time." Webb stopped talking and listened intently, seeking the source of a muted sound within the ship. It did not come again and Webb opened his fingers to let the paper fall away. He rested his hands on the railing of the upper bunk.

"That floater was a fraud."

"Oh, was it?" Kate asked politely.

"You know it was—you knew it for a fake long before I did. Calkins or that courier told you. Amarillo rigged that ship to resemble a derelict and sent it up to intercept me; somebody behind Amarillo wanted to put the courier on board this bucket. Somebody wanted to put him on board as desperately as you wanted on, back there in Toronto. As desperately as you worked to get back on while I was orbiting." His mocking grin was entirely devoid of mirth. "This old tub turns out to be pretty popular, like it was a pot of gold or something."

"I find it an interesting ship."

"I find it a rusty one. Why did you want on board?"

"To visit the Tombaugh."

"You didn't know where I was going. Bull!"

"That is a most vulgar habit, Mr. Webb."

"I have lots of vulgar habits—like this one."

Bristol saw it coming but it wasn't at all what she expected and the questing hand caught her off guard. Webb reached out carefully, unbelligerently, to touch her body. The gentle hand explored her breasts.

She jerked away from him. "I will grant any man that first pass, Webb. You've just had it. Don't touch me again."

He nodded with tough satisfaction. "Good! Now we're down to bedrock—let's keep it that way. That wasn't a pass, Bristol. I wanted to see where you hid it."

"Hid what?"

"The telemeter gimmick—the thing that loused up my radar."

"I have no telemeter gimmick, whatever that may be."

"You had one until the courier took it."

"You are mistaken."

"I wasn't mistaken about that fouled screen—Torcon wasn't mistaken about theirs. You had a telemeter."

"I did not." She saw his fingers curling on the bunk railing and knew the culmination was coming. It could no longer be avoided.

Webb said bleakly, "You are a police agent."

"I am not."

"You're a police agent," he repeated with naked hatred. "You can't pin a murder rap on Jimmy Cross so you're trying to pin it on me. You refuse to believe that stupid kid killed himself and now you want me to hang for it."

"I am *not* a police agent."

"Liar!" Webb leaped at her.

The auto pilot echoed his shout with a soft burring sound as the tapes eased off and stopped, killing the drive. The *Xanthus* went into free fall as Webb leaped, catching him by wild surprise. He realized too late what the muted, unidentified sound had been.

Webb shot over the rim of the bunk, unable to control his trajectory and his head butted the woman in the stomach. Bristol gasped with pain and parted her lips to suck in air. She twisted from beneath his thrashing body and managed to sit up. The movement shoved him backward. Webb threw out both hands to catch himself, caught the railing and then climbed into the bunk with her, clawing at the concealing cloth.

"Let's see what you're hiding, sister!"

She put a hard fist into his face and pushed, but he rolled away and lunged again, intent on the open neckline of the creamy coveralls. Bristol swung with an uppercut, laying open the side of his jaw. Webb's bellow thundered about the cabin. The blow had propelled him backward but as his flying body shot away his fingers caught at the cloth, tearing open her suit to the waistline. Bristol's carefully simulated skin disease was revealed to his startled gaze.

His feet struck the opposite wall and he used the wall as a springboard, driving himself toward the bunk again. Webb came over the rail in eager desire and fell into the fury of her anger. She hit him in the face with a short, savage thrust, repeated it, and followed that with a side-hand stroke aimed at his exposed throat. Webb opened his mouth to say, "Damn—" and she kicked him in the stomach with every pound of strength she could muster. He cried out in sudden agony. His body zoomed across the cabin a second time and smashed against the bulkhead. Dull red droplets from his crushed nose drifted gently toward the air intake.

Bristol sprang from the bunk, miscalculated her leap and fell on him, carrying his unconscious body to the deck.

Presently the engines resumed their deceleration firing, again without forewarning.

Irvin Webb opened his eyes and saw the sagging webwork of the bunk above him. He realized his passenger was in the bunk, but he couldn't care less. Only dimly conscious of his motions, he put a hand against the hull and listened to the operating ship. The movement caused a painful reaction throughout the network of muscles in his abdomen and he let the hand fall to the bunk. He was loosely strapped down.

His muttered, "Hell and Jehoshaphat, woman, what did you do to me?" was blurred and indistinct because his lips wouldn't function properly.

From above she answered. "In your own colorful language, Webb, I damned near killed you."

Slowly, with pain overriding every small action, Webb opened the straps and rolled over on his stomach. He was stopped there because the searing agony in his lower regions demanded a cessation of movement. After a long while he raised his head to stare at the chronometer but it was only a distant, unfocussed blur. Abruptly he was sick.

"Bristol?"

She came out of the upper bunk and landed with a lithe grace beside him. "Yes, Webb?"

"Can't see the chronometer. What does it read?" Webb was stunned when she told him. Again he unbuckled the belt to climb out and again he felt sickness rising in him.

She pushed him back. "Stay there."

"No time, damn you! Dead orbit coming."

"The tapes will take care of the orbit, Webb."

"Like hell they will! We're fifty seconds late; the stinking jackleg did that." His aching tongue stopped the flow of words and it was many minutes before he could speak again. "Whipped by a woman," was the mournful whisper.

"First and last time, I hope. You weren't a pretty sight. But I did manage to feed you a little."

"Gotta get up. Beat that dead orbit." Webb pulled himself from the bunk and then clung to the stanchion. Sickness filled his mouth but he forced it down again. His legs wobbled, threatening to dump him on the deck. "Give me a hand."

"Get back in the bunk, or else this ship will land a dead man on the Tombaugh."

"If I can't get to that manual this bucket will spill us all over the Tombaugh—stupid fool. I said we're running fifty seconds late."

"You've said it several times. And it means a difference of only a hundred and fifty miles."

Webb put a hand over his eyes to shut out the light. "Hundred and fifty miles affects my orbit," he told her wearily. "Knocks the hell out of it. We always come in on target over the trailing limb, and the trailing limb marks the perigee. When the tapes put us into orbit Pluto will be a hundred and fifty miles farther away." He had to stop again, waiting for breath and for strength. "We'll be dancing in the damndest orbit ever! Too wild and too wide. And the devil only knows what the apogee will be."

"But what are you trying to do?"

"Bring it in on manual. Change orbit. Figure the deceleration and find a new orbit. Then keep right on orbiting until I can find the Tombaugh and set her down."

"I *thought* you were being overly melodramatic," she replied cheerfully. "We *can* land on the Tombaugh, after all. I have confidence in you, Webb."

He seemed to find that funny but the weak attempt at laughter was no more than a choking gurgle. "Oh, hell no, there's nothing to worry about. Nothing at all. Do you suppose they'll wait for us?"

"Who?"

"Those jokers on the Tombaugh? Those star-peeps sweating out their new gear? How long do you think they'll sit there, watching us whirl around over their heads? A week? Two weeks? Damn it, woman, I have to *find* a favorable orbit to get near them, and I have to *find* the Tombaugh plateau to land on—without coming down smack on top of their lousy telescopes."

"But you know where it is, you've been there."

"I've always found it with updated tapes, you stupid idiot. I've always orbited by the tape and sat down by the tape. I've never hit the Tombaugh *wild* before." He relapsed into the choking, feeble laughter. *"I know where it is —I've been there.* Bristol, you stink."

His legs buckled, throwing him to the deck.

Kate Bristol picked him up and carried him to the board. There was no chair for him to sit in so she had to hold him there.

The aged freighter lifted over the trailing limb of Pluto, climbing away from perigee and beginning its seventy-second circuit of the frozen planet. Below it, somewhere on the barren wastes, the radio tower alongside the Tombaugh Station hurled a steady guidance signal into the skies. As the *Xanthus* cleared the horizon, voice signals resumed, offered up by the personnel of the half dozen ships already nesting on the plateau.

"Webb—hey there, Webb, ain't you ever coming down?"

"Shut up, Busby," Webb retorted. "I'm sweating."

"Sweating!' the master of the *Yandro* whooped. And to all those listening he added, "Webb's got a woman up there —he's afraid to bring her down and let us look-see."

"Come on, Webb, you can't stay up there forever."

"Tell you what," said a new voice, "give him an even hundred passes and then we'll shoot him down."

"Send the woman down, Webb. You stay there."

"Shuddup!" Webb roared at them. "Busby—you there? Listen, Busby, I figured two more passes and I can pull her tail feathers. Lend a hand now."

The voices fell silent and Busby was heard again. "Sure, Webb. Come on in—they want your gear."

Watching the chronometer and listening to the guidance signal from the plateau, Webb poised an expectant thumb over the firing button and waited. The bucket hurtled tail first along its useless orbit, driving now for the ridiculous apogee. Webb hung over the board, his nerves taut. He was no longer conscious of the woman behind him, holding him there. At that moment when the radio signal reached its peak and broke he stabbed at the button, holding it down four seconds. The engines burst into brief and noisy life and then they were done, throwing the vessel back into free fall in a new orbit.

The four seconds had been painful, sharply reminding him of his battered groin and he was grateful for the respite when they were over. The radio signal faded as the ship passed over the far horizon. Webb's head sank to his chest and he rediscovered the arms around him.

"Brace yourself, Bristol. Rough one coming up."

"I'm ready, Webb. Good luck."

"Luck!" was the muttered reply.

The *Xanthus* rounded the planet and shot for the new horizon, seeking the feeble light of the distant sun. It lifted over the trailing limb of Pluto, climbing away from perigee and beginning the seventy-fourth circuit of the ice-locked world. The radio signal came in loud.

"Webb," the voice reached his ears, "you're over the horizon on a direct line. Keep it there." A short period of tense silence. "Soon now, Webb. You're skinning the ice mountains. Set up your trim."

"Not yet—not yet. I've got eighteen seconds."

"I don't think so, Webb. Less than fifteen from the line of it."

"Eighteen here, Busby. Figured down to the decimal."

The freighter plunged heavily onward, climbing out of perigee in a shallow arc and soaring without sound to a high point above the Tombaugh tower. Webb trimmed the cold jets fore and aft, setting up for positional change. He watched the chronometer and kept an ear tuned to the beeping signal, calculating the precise instant the tone would break. Sweat beaded his forehead and blurred his vision.

"Webb?" the nervous talker broke in."

"Six seconds," Webb flung back at the ground.

"I think you're overshooting, Webb."

"Now five, four, three, two, one—" and he rammed his thumb down on the firing button, unwittingly cursing it in his anxiety to drive it home. The engines hesitated and then coughed when they should have flamed.

"Webb, damn you, goose it!"

Webb pushed the harder, seeking inanely to recapture the lost moment. The vacillating engines fired. His free hand swept out and punched for the jet trim and then he clung to the board, knowing the jolt that was coming. The woman clung to him, bracing him. The shock came when the old ship reared skyward and then sat down on its flaming tail, riding it down. Webb hung on and watched the radar screen.

Busby screamed at him. "Webb—*overshoot!*"

"Pull out!" someone else bellowed in his ears. "Pull your trim or you'll hit the rocks. Pull out now!"

Webb stared at the screen and discovered the plateau and its huddle of ships far to starboard. The Tombaugh and its radio tower jutted up behind them. Savagely, quickly, with the instinctive movement born of naked fear, Webb worked the jets and sought to turn the ship on its axis, parallel to the ground below him. He felt the cold jets firing, exerting a minute lift on the vessel, and then the still flaming tail section struck a mountain peak. A harsh buckling sound reverberated through the ship.

Webb clung to the board, knowing the worst had hit him. He felt a shudder run through the hull, accompanied by a drumming crack even in the absence of an outside atmosphere, and the entire tail section of the bucket fell away. The engines were lost. The freighter paused and seemed to hang suspended, and then dropped. The man and woman toppled to the pitching deck, both of them grabbing for any handhold to offer itself.

The *Xanthus* fell on the rugged slope of the mountain that had speared it and rolled with sickening motion, tumbling downward until it struck and ricocheted off a boulder pack at the bottom. The portside tanks splintered and fell away. Still pushed by its own momentum, the freighter skidded wildly across an unseen shoreline and then shot outward over a sea of frozen methane. A great rock thrusting up through the sea ripped the ship from bow to stern, scattering cargo over the ice. The *Xanthus* skidded wildly across the sea.

Against a sky rich with stars the distant sun was a bright giant, an incredibly large and brilliant star but yet one without a perceptible disc. It cast a puny light over the packed snow and marked a dull reflection on the frozen sea. Near at hand slim needles of rock jutted up through the ice while beyond the needles and beyond the alien sea, an unknown number of miles away, massive mountain ranges ringed the horizon and built up solid white peaks to catch the meager sunlight. The little world was motionless and deathly still.

She could look back along their path and distinguish dark objects scattered in the wake; she could see the sun, remote and barely friendly, lying now in a shallow dish between two mountain crags; she could glance about her and see a world which had not changed—except for a mote known as the Tombaugh Station—in all the years that man had known it existed. She turned and stared at the wretched hulk behind her. The wreck of the *Xanthus* was beached well above the shoreline of a nameless island, twisted and broken in crazy fashion. The full sunlight enabled her to pick out the name painted on the hull.

She stared down at her radio, resting on a rock. If they were fortunate its clamoring signal could be heard.

Kate Bristol clambered over the wreckage and entered the ship, pulling the hatch snug behind her. Darkness enveloped the cabin, for which she was thankful. That tiny portion of the vessel was still tight.

"Bristol?"

"Are you still alive? Are you unkillable, Webb?" She inched along the unseen deck until she found his body. "I was afraid your suit had ripped."

"What were you doing outside?"

"Setting up my radio. A distress signal, Webb, not a telemeter gimmick."

"Radio," he repeated thoughtfully. "Well—maybe."

She understood his meaning. "We shouldn't be too difficult to find."

"Maybe," he said again and lapsed into silence.

"Try to stay awake; it's very cold in here."

"Still want to hang me, cop?" There was no rancor.

"For the last time, Webb: I am not a police agent. I was put aboard for a purpose, but not a police purpose."

"Who else is interested?" he asked cynically.

"Your insurance company. And what a loss *this is!*"

Webb stared into the blackness above him. "Ah!" The sound carried many subtle meanings. "They don't want to pay off for Singleton's death—they're going to screw me out of my break-off money!"

Bristol said, "They don't intend to pay a beneficiary who happens to be a murderer."

"What's the difference? You've tapped me."

"Wrong again, Webb. I've tapped Jimmy Cross."

"*Bull.*" The two words ran together sounded like one.

"Please stop using that vulgar term." She located his shoulder on the deck near her knee and tapped it for emphasis. "Listen to this, Webb. I am going to say it once and only once. It makes little difference whether you choose to believe it or not; I don't have to convince you, only my superiors.

"James Cross deliberately rigged your auto pilot to cause Singleton's death, and to cause yours as well. If you weren't such a stubborn idiot you would have discovered that for yourself, as I did. Time and again, Webb, you were taken by surprise when the tapes stopped or started without giving prior warning. You were caught off guard when you leaped the rail for me, and went into free fall."

"Old age—the damn ship was falling apart."

"It has fallen apart," she pointed out. "But the auto pilot was given a helpful push. I found a printed circuit in the base of that machine, and I found a short loop of thinly insulated wire touching a part of the circuit. I think you call the wire a jumper. The jumper had been so placed that it rubbed against one channel; insulation had burned off the jumper at that point and the channel had burned through. Your warning system operated fitfully at first, Webb, and then it failed to operate at all. I have also read your ship's manuals and the diagrams. There should be no jumper at that point."

"When the hell did you do all that?"

'While you were visiting the derelict, and again while you lay unconscious in your bunk a few hours ago. I know what I am saying, Webb. Your partner sabotaged the ship."

"It could be a patching job," he said thinly.

"It was a patching job, a most ingenious patching job. But there's more, Webb. I did something more while you were visiting the derelict. I experimented with the drain valves. I tried in every possible manner to trip both levers simultaneously, using only one hand and arm—even using one leg and foot. It is impossible. The levers are positioned in such a manner that it is impossible. You would have realized that if you weren't so insistent on branding Singleton a dunce. A simultaneous flushing can be accomplished only by using both hands, or by a man falling across them. A man standing in the cubicle could be caught off guard, and be knocked across the levers."

She felt Webb's body stiffen with surprise.

"You're catching on, Webb. Singleton died because he lacked your experience. You warned me when time was drawing near to quit the orbit, you knew by the feel and the sounds what was to happen. But Singleton lacked your experience, and perhaps your common sense, and when the device failed that first time he was trapped and thrown. It was his terrible bad luck to be in the cubicle when it failed." She shook her head, forgetting that he could not see in the darkness. "Not you, Webb. Jimmy Cross. My report will name Jimmy Cross."

Webb broke the silence. "I'm sorry, Bristol."

"No apologies accepted. I bought my passage."

"You've got a refund coming," he said with faint bitterness. "Everybody's got a refund coming." When she said nothing to that, he asked, "What do you think of the place —outside?"

"I want to go home," she answered truthfully.

"Me, too." He squirmed on the deck, seeking but not finding a more comfortable position. "Wish to hell I could sit up."

"Stay where you are. There is some heavy object pinning your legs. We need a rescue party."

"If it comes," Webb grunted, and knew why he had lost all sense of feeling in his legs. He wondered blackly if he would also lose his legs. "Grounded, dammit."

"I suggest that you stay home, after this debacle."

"Last trip—I've got break-off money."

After a time he asked wearily, "Hear anything on your radio? Mine's busted."

"I thought I heard voices a bit ago. I'm not sure."

"Say, Bristol?"

"Yes, Webb?"

"Where did you hide that distress radio?"

"Don't be naive, Webb."

Webb dozed off and then became aware of what he was doing. He jerked himself awake with a start.

"Maybe we'll run into each other again," he offered hopefully. His moving fingers found her knee.

"I doubt that very much," Bristol said and moved the knee.

The last man in the world doesn't necessarily have to sit alone in a room waiting for a knock at the door. Only an unimaginative clod would do that.

The last man in the world who still retained his wits, and his wit, would roam about the town doing all those things he could not do when it was inhabited. The high prices of groceries and clothing would mean nothing, and inflation would be only a bygone nightmare. All would be open to his indulgence: luxury hotels, stores, theaters, banks and automobiles. If the last man in the world chanced across a faithful companion he could live in contentment to a ripe old age.

TO A RIPE OLD AGE

GEORGE YOUNG SNEEZED AND SQUINTED HIS eyes. The dirty wallpaper clinging to the ceiling above him seemed ready to come loose and fall. He sneezed again and rolled his eyes slowly, taking in the equally sad paper peeling from the sidewalls—faded roses, and beneath that, blue feathers. A battered old telephone hung on the wall near the door. The room contained a peculiar odor. His trousers were thrown over a chair beside the bed.

"Mother of Moses!" George Young complained aloud. "Another firetrap."

He fought away the ache in his back and the dull pain in his chest to sit up. The movement sent a fine cloud of dust flying. He sneezed again, and continued sneezing until the dust had cleared away.

"What the hell goes on here?" George demanded of the peeling wallpaper. His uneasy nostrils cringed from the smell of the place.

Slowly swinging his feet off the bed and to the floor, he swore loudly when his naked toes made jarring contact with several glass bottles. Curious, George peered down. Liquor bottles—all empty. With growing incredulity he examined them, attempted to count them. Bottles, all shapes, all kinds, all colors, all manner and variety of labels, empty bottles. They began at the baseboard of the wall near the head of his bed and marched across the dusty carpet, a reasonably straight line of them running from the head to the foot of the bed. His eyes swung that way, still doubtfully counting, to find the bottles turned a corner. At the count of 52 they swung around the scarred bedpost and continued parallel with the footboard.

George gingerly lifted himself to his feet and rested his hands on the footboard, staring over and down. The empty bottles continued their fantastic march across the floor and turned a second corner. George swallowed and lay back down on the bed. Dust flew. He sneezed.

"Stop that, damn it!" he yelled hoarsely. "Why don't they dust this stinking firetrap?"

After a long moment he very carefully rolled over on his belly to stare at the floor on the opposite side of the bed. Empty bottles. After turning that second corner the bottles maintained their marching line up to the wallboard once more. His bed was ringed by bottles, a three-sided ring with each end anchored at the wall. All empty, all large—he saw that he had not wasted his money on pint sizes.

"Money—!"

Alarmed, George leaped from the bed in another cloud of dust to snatch up the rumpled trousers. There was no wallet in the pockets. He shook his addled head to clear away the dust and haze, and grabbed for the pillow. The wallet was there. Hurriedly he opened it, plucked out the sheaf of currency and counted the remaining bills.

"Oh, no, Mother of Moses!" Thoughtlessly, George ran to the window, inserted his fingers into the two-inch opening along the bottom and pulled it up. He thrust his head out into the hot sunlight. "Police! I've been robbed!"

He brought his head in again to stare at the array of bottles. Once more he counted the money in his wallet. He lifted a naked foot to kick at the nearest empty, and thought the better of it. Slowly then, using a dirty index finger, he made a second count of the number of bottles, multiplied the total by five, and compared that sum with the remaining money. The answer was startling.

"I was robbed," he repeated dully. "Hell, I never get that drunk! Why—I *couldn't* drink all that." George paused to survey the marching line. "I don't think I could." He paused again, considering. "Well, I never could before."

He stepped over the bottles and sat down on the bed. Dust arose, he sneezed. The single bedsheet beneath him was covered with a crust that made his bottom itch. The wallet lay open in his hand.

More than $400 gone . . . where? Into all that joy-juice? Four hundred bucks, the money he had saved up for his furlough. Four hundred bucks earned the hard way by scrubbing latrines, polishing brass, cleaning the damned rifle, policing the grounds, drilling, drilling, drilling. . . . Eleven months in the army, eleven months of deepest privation and degrading toil, eleven months of saving his meager pay and running it up in crap and poker games; and finally, after eleven months, a ten-day delay-enroute. From Fort Dix, New Jersey, to Camp Walton, California, with a delay-enroute.

All right, so he had delayed enroute. Somewhere. He had climbed down off the train—in somewhere town—and squandered about $400 on those bottles now surrounding the bed. But where was somewhere town? And still more alarming was a new thought: which of those ten days was it *now*, today? How far was he from Camp Walton and how many days had he left to reach there?

Hurriedly he arose from the bed in a cloud of dust and jumped the line of bottles, to snatch up the earpiece of the ancient wallphone. There was a layer of dust on it.

"Hey, down there!" George shouted into its mouth, "where the hell is this? And what day is it?"

The phone stayed dead.

"Hell of a note," he declared and let the earpiece bang against the wall. Behind the faded wallpaper some loose plaster dribbled down. "Hell of a note, I say." He turned to appraise the room.

The room was dingy like all cheap hotels, the carpet was ragged and worn as in all firetraps and the bed was a hand-me-down the Salvation Army had thrown away. He looked at the discolored sheet and wondered how he had slept on it, sniffed the odor of the room and wondered how he had stayed alive in it. His body itched, so he scratched. His chest seemed to be encrusted and matted with a sticky, odorous glue. The glue had a familiar smell. Dust covered the bed other than where he had lain, covered the solitary chair and the light fixture hanging from the ceiling. Dust arose from the carpet as he stalked across it. George paused once more to examine the bottles—a thin layer of dust covered the bottles.

"Hell of a note," he repeated and picked up his trousers. He shook the garment, sneezed twice, and put them on. He couldn't find his socks, shoes or shirt—there was nothing in the room other than his trousers. Wearing them, he unlocked the bedroom door to stare at the number. He was on the third floor. Without hesitation he strode into the hallway and sought the stairs, dust flying with every footfall. George clumped down the stairs, taking a savage delight in making as much noise as possible, navigated the second floor landing and continued on to the street floor. The lobby was empty.

"Hey there! Wake up—it's me, George Young."

There was no answer, no sudden appearance.

George strode over to the tiny desk and pounded on it. Dust flew up in his nostrils and he sneezed again. He glanced around the lobby to discover he was still alone. A calendar pad caught his eye and he whirled it around, blew dust from the surface and read the date.

"The sixteenth," he repeated it aloud. "That was . . . uh, two days after I left Dix. Yeah. The sixteenth . . . so I've got eight days left anyhow." He pounded on the desk once more and waited several minutes for an answer. The sunlight shining through the unwashed glass of the street door finally caught his eyes, and he turned toward it.

George Young pushed out into the bright sun, stood on the hot pavement to stare at the empty street.

"What the hell goes on here?" he demanded.

A collie dog pushed up from the back seat of a nearby automobile, regarded him with some surprise, and leaped out to trot over to him.

"Well—hello, George!" the dog greeted him warmly. "Mother of Moses, am I glad to see you up and around. I am your best friend, George."

"Go to hell," George snapped peevishly and pivoted on the sidewalk to stare both ways along the deserted street. "Where is—" He broke off, whirled back to the dog.

"*What* did you say?"

"I said," the animal repeated happily, "that I am your best friend. You know—a dog is man's best friend. I am a dog and you are a man, so I am your best friend."

George stared suspiciously at the collie's shining eyes, its open mouth and lolling pink tongue. Then he very carefully backed across the sidewalk and into the lobby, pulling shut the door. The dog padded after him and put its nose to the glass.

"Open the door, George. I am your best friend."

"Nooo . . . not mine, you ain't. Go away."

"But George, I *am* so. You told me."

"I didn't tell you nothing . . . now scat!"

"You did, George, you *did*," the animal insisted. There was something akin to pleading in its voice. "This is a hell of a note! You were upstairs sleeping on the bed and I came up to see you every day. You taught me to speak,

George, you said you didn't want any dumb dogs hanging around. You taught me everything I know."

"I don't bark," George declared hotly.

"You said it was the English language, George, whatever that is. Good old King's English, you told me. Is King a man too, George? You said a dog was man's best friend, so here I am a dog, eager to be your best friend."

George fixed the collie with a beady eye. "I never saw a talking dog before."

The dog giggled. "I never saw a talking man before. Gee whiz, but you stinked."

"Where are they?" George demanded then. "Where is everybody? Where'd they go?"

"Alas, they were all gone when I arrived."

George Young jumped and searched the visible parts of the street outside, and then whirled around for another inspection of the lobby. He was the sole remaining human in sight. He glared down at the dog, summoned his courage and pushed through the lobby door a second time to stand on the burning pavement. He made a careful survey of the street.

Automobiles stood at the curb before the hotel and were parked elsewhere along the street. None contained an occupant. Office windows and shop doorways were open to the warm summer air, quite empty of life. Debris littered the streets and avenues, moving only on the occasional prompting of some idle breeze. Tall buildings reared along the block, uninhabited. There was no sound but his own hoarse breathing. The thoroughfares were empty, the cars empty, the stores and offices empty, the lobby behind him empty. He saw no people—George chopped off the train of thought to glance into the air, to search the ledges running along the nearer buildings. There were no birds, either. Nothing, no one, but him and the collie.

"Where is everybody?" he asked again, weakly.

"Gone," the dog told him sadly, echoing his emotions. "Alas, all gone, absent without leave, over the hill, taking a powder, vamoosed. Hell of a note."

"But *where?*" the bewildered soldier insisted.

The collie tried and failed to shrug. "Gobbled up."

George growled at him. "You're pretty damned sassy for a dog."

"I am your best friend, George," said the collie. "I came up to see you every day."

"You're nuts. The door was locked."

"Oh no, George. I flew. I am your best friend."

The soldier contemplated the dog with a weary disgust. "So all right . . . so you flew. If you can sit there and argue with me, I guess you can fly." And then he added triumphantly: "But I was asleep all the time, so how could I teach you anything?"

"Mother of Moses, George, it all came forth from your mind! Oh yes, you were asleep all right, hitting the sack, rolling in the hay, taking 40 and whatnot, but the King's English flowed right out of your mind. Everything I am today I owe to your mind, brain, gray matter, skull-stuffing, sawdust and et cetera. You didn't explain et cetera to me, George. All the while you slept your mind flowed, flowed right out to me in brainwaves. I know it all, I know everything you know. I am your best friend, George, because you said a dog was man's best friend."

The man stared, incredulous. "Do you mean to say you flew upstairs and *read* my mind while I slept?"

"That I did, George, that I did. You smelled, George. We were in perfect sync, fix, communion, tune."

"Oh, brother!"

"Am I really your brother, George?" The collie's tail wagged with sudden pleasure. "Yes, I guess I am your brother. You said once you were a son of a—" The dog yelped with pain and jumped away. "Now, George!"

"Don't you *now-George* me! Get away from here, go on, shoo. I don't like talking dogs."

"You shouldn't treat your best friend that way, George old pal, bosom buddy, good stick."

He lunged savagely at the animal. "You ain't my best friend—not by a long shot! I don't make friends with talking dogs. I don't make friends with smart-aleck dogs. I don't make friends with flying dogs. I don't ever want to see you again! Now get out of here before I kick your—" and he sent the kick flying. The frightened collie yelped and scuttled away, to look back just once before vanishing into an alley.

George Young left the hotel behind and strode with a determined purpose to the nearer intersection. Standing at the corner, he raised a hand to shade his eyes from the sun and peer along the four streets. His determination dribbled away. No living thing moved in his line of sight. Down the block a car had gone out of control, veered across the sidewalk and smashed into a store window. He ran to it hopefully, prepared to welcome nothing more than the body of some unlucky motorist. The car was empty, save for a crumpled newspaper.

"The bomb!" he shouted aloud at the sudden thought. "The dirty bastards dropped the bomb. They wiped—" His voice trailed away to nothing as he examined the nearer buildings. None of them showed the slightest traces of a blast, any blast. There was nothing to indicate so small a thing as a black powder bomb going off. Defeated, he reached into the car for the newspaper and smoothed it out.

It held no mention of a bomb, no hint, or threat of a bomb, no clue or forewarning to any sort of a catastrophe. The front page as well as those inside mirrored nothing more than the day-to-day violence at home and abroad. Like the dusty calendar on the hotel desk, the newspaper was dated the sixteenth. A stopping date. He dropped it, uncomprehending. "Hell of a note," George complained.

Why . . . you'd think he was the last man in the world.

George Young sat on the curb in front of a grocery store, watching the summer sun go down and eating his supper from a collection of pilfered cans and jars. He had helped himself to the food, there being no one in the store to serve him or restrain him. The bread he had passed by because it was hard and some of the loaves showed traces of green mold, and that in turn caused him to doubt the fruits and vegetables. Most of the meats and cheeses in a neutralized refrigerator seemed to be safe, but still it held a peculiar odor and he had slammed the door on the box.

Cans, jars and a box of wax-sealed crackers made up his meal. Unable to locate a coffee pot or running water, he drank canned juices and soda water.

In the several hours since leaving the hotel he had also helped himself to an automobile and wandered the length and breadth of the town, looking for someone, anyone. He had left the car radio running for hours, waiting for a voice, any voice, child, man or woman. The only moving thing he had seen was a flea-bitten sparrow that faithfully followed his wanderings, clearly chirping "George—" at tiresome intervals. He had thrown a rock at the sparrow. The day was gone and empty, the sun setting on a lonesome city and a lonesome man.

"Hell of a note!" he cried for the hundredth time, and

hurled an empty can far across the street. It rattled loudly
in the deserted silence. The silence puzzled him, frightened
him, made him unsure of his future. Should he drive on to
Camp Walton—would he find anyone living in California?
What about tomorrow, and the next day, and all the days
after that? What would it be like to be alone for the rest
of his life?

"Hell of a note," he said again, shouting after the can.
"Just one woman would do. One lousy woman!"

"Georgie, lamb. . . ."

He stiffened with surprise and swiveled his head on his
shoulders. She stood waiting only a few feet away, a vision
for his starving eyes. He toppled from the curb with shock
and lay in the street, looking up at her. Wow, what a woman!

She possessed the shape of all those lovely, desirable girls
in the pin-up pictures he treasured, only more shapely. Her
hair was the glorious color of flaming ripe wheat to match
the glowing descriptions he had read in a thousand stories,
only more glorious. She had a face so breathtakingly beautiful it defied description; eyes like limpid, inviting pools
that heroes tumbled into. She was a tall, long-legged,
chesty, tanned babe with enough sizzle for five harem
dancers. And she was clad in nothing more than a skimpy
two-piece swim suit.

Her every line and curve, hollow and hill shrieked a
precious commodity which George was always seeking. She
had shining golden eyes and a lolling, pink tongue. She was
what that guy Smith would describe as a seven-sector call-
out. And now she waited there all alone, appealing to him!
George struggled up from the gutter.

"Honey . . . baby . . . ," she seemed to whisper.

"Mother of Moses!" George declared. "All mine!"

"Lamb-pie, angel child . . . come to mama." She held out
her hands to him.

"Where in hell did *you* come from?" he demanded.

"Oh, I've been around, George. Are you lonely?"

"Am I lonely!" he shouted, and leaped the curb to put
his hands on her. "Baby, where have you been all my life?"

She smiled up into his happy face. "Oh, I'm from Glissix,
George, but you don't really care about that. I came here a
few days ago. I'm a floozy."

George froze. "Say that again?"

"I'm a floozy, George, a skirt, a doll, a walker, a babe. Do you like me, George? Do you like my skin?"

He raised the palm of his hand to slap his forehead rapidly, knocking out the cobwebs. She was still there. "Look," he pleaded. "I don't get all this. I don't care a damn where you came from and I don't give a damn what you are. You're *people,* and you look like a million to me. All I know is that you're the hottest peach I ever laid eyes on in my life, and I'm craving company." He held onto her arm tightly lest she vanish. "Let's get together. How about a drink?"

"Drink? But I don't need water, George."

"Who said anything about water? Look, doll, you *must* know the score, you've seen what this town is like. There ain't nobody here—the whole damned population has skipped out and left us. Mass desertion, that's what it is. The place is ours, see? All we have to do is walk along and help ourselves." He tugged at her arm to start her moving. "Look down there—see that saloon? That's for us. And over in the next block is another one, and another one. All ours. We just help ourselves, doll, free and on the house. Come on, let's you and me have a nip of rotgut."

She was trotting alongside him now to match his eager, rapid pace. "Will I like rotgut, George?"

"Baby, you'll love it!" he told her gustily, watching the jiggle of her garments from the corner of his eye. "It can *do* things for you."

It did things for her.

Dusk had long since fallen and the moon was up, but it failed to top the taller buildings and illuminate the street canyons until near midnight. At that hour, George and the lovely doll had passed freely from the portal of one liquid refreshment to the next, sampling this and that, all unaware of the growing darkness and the absence of electricity. They were only aware of their interest in each other. And rotgut had done some startling things to the blonde whose hair was like ripe wheat. For one thing, the hair exhibited a certain difficulty in maintaining the color of ripe wheat. Had the various saloons been illuminated by electricity the carousing soldier might have noticed that, might have noticed that the hair was sometimes reddish, sometimes brown, sometimes like long green grass and sometimes no color at all.

And for another thing, demon rum had caused the girl to be acutely aware of the confining garments she wore. They were an uncomfortable restraint and she soon slipped out of them. "I'm not used to wearing clothes, George," she said by way of explanation.

George grandly waved the explanation aside, and the upper half of the swim suit now reposed on the antlers of a buck hanging on some lost wall behind them. The lower half he carried in his hip pocket as a souvenir. He had offered to remove his trousers, the only article of clothing he now possessed, but he said he was afraid of catching cold. And somewhere, sometime during the night George discovered the moonlight spilling in the window.

"Come here, buttercup," he said, reaching for her hand. "I want to see how you sparkle in the moonlight."

He turned and marched away with the hand. The girl got up from her chair as quickly as she could and followed it. He paused at the window, to place her in the proper position and her body sparkled in the moonlight. The moon seemed to make it sparkle a bit queerly, as though seen through a haze or a curtain of smoky cellophane. George decided they needed another drink to dispel the illusions. He usually played bartender because she was unfamiliar with the liquids and had mixed some devilish concoctions.

"I ain't been drunk for a long, *long* time," George confided to her, thumping her shoulder with each word. "Not since last night in fact. I counted the bottles—man, what bottles! Only you know what?" He hesitated, groping for the half-remembered details of the episode. "You know what?"

"What?" the sparkling body asked.

He reached for the body, picked her up and placed her on the bar before him. "Gee, you don't weigh a thing." He was pleased with his unexpected strength, and slapped her thigh. "But you sure got what it takes."

"What?" she asked again, smoothing out the indentation his hand had made.

"I didn't really drink all those bottles—no sir! I thought I did, this morning, but I didn't really." He stopped again to collect the memories. "We was talking about those champagne baths, see? Me and some of the guys on the train. One of the guys, this corporal, said he read a piece in the paper about an actress or somebody taking a bath in champagne, and another guy pushes in and says no, it was a tub of milk. They got to arguing about it and to shut them up, I said I'd take a whiskey bath and see how it was. That's what I said." He paused for breath, took a drink and maneuvered a restless hand. "So I did, see honey? I bought all those bottles, must have spent over 400 bucks and got myself all those bottles."

"And took a bath," she finished for him. "Baby."

"Naw, I didn't take a bath! I couldn't—there wasn't no bathtub in my room. So I just laid down on the bed and poured it over me. Of course, I drank *some* you understand, but I poured it over me. Took a whiskey shower, by damn! Four hundred bucks worth, right on me." George reached down to scratch the dried glue on his chest. "That's why I'm all sticky." He marvelled at himself. "Boy . . . I'll bet I smelled this morning!"

"You certainly did, George. I visited you every day."

"You did? You really did? Do you mean to tell me that I laid there like a log with a hot peach like you in the room? I must be going crazy!"

"Oh, I didn't mind at all, George. I thought you were nice. I am your best—I want to do things with you honey, lamb-pie, sweet man, snuggles."

"Atta gal!" He pinched her but she made no protest. "You're the kind of a doll I go for. I'm glad there ain't no people around here—just me and you, all alone. More fun that way."

"Alas, they are all gone, George. Skedaddled. They've been gone for many days. The Hunters ate them . . . gobbled them up." She sipped at a bottle of rotgut and delightful shivers ran down her body.

"Yeah," he said, watching the shivers and the body. "That's what a dumb dog told me this morning. Everybody gone, except me and you." He swallowed another drink. "Ate them all up, eh? Imagine that, just like cannibals. What hunters?"

"The Hunters from Glissix."

"Never heard of the place. Is it in Jersey?"

"No, George." She shook her head slowly because the rotgut was playing tricks with her equipoise. "Glissix is up there."

"Up where?" he asked the lone reflection in the mirror.

She lifted a slow, lazy arm to point toward the moonlit sky. "Up there." George wasn't watching the arm, he had only moved his head to observe the effect on her chest.

"Glissix is out there," she continued, "away out there beyond the moon and the sun, George. Out there and far away; it's dark and cold and not like *here* at all, it's more like the moonplace, honeyboy. You wouldn't like Glissix, my hero, pet, joyboy, sweetguy."

"Never heard of the town," he declared and opened another bottle by striking its neck against the bar. "Have a nip of this . . . do you a world of good. From Glissix, eh? Are you a Hunter? Hunter-ess?"

"Oh no, George!" She played with his hair. "I can't be a Hunter . . . the Hunters eat living things, like you. I don't eat *living* things, George. I'm a Follower."

"Pleased to meet'cha, follower. I don't know what I am; I ain't voted yet. What did them hunters want to gobble up the people for, babydoll?"

The blonde babydoll leaned forward from her seat on the bar to wrap her legs about his waist and a friendly arm around his shoulders. The arm proved a trifle short because the rotgut was playing tricks on her again, so she lengthened it to stretch all the way around to the opposite shoulder. Babydoll placed her inviting pink lips against his and spoke while she was kissing him. The kiss had a curious dry quality.

"They were hungry, lamb-pie. They always wake up hungry, every spring. And they go everywhere, eating everything that is alive. All summer long they eat, eat, eat, making themselves fat so they can sleep all winter. Sometimes I go hungry too, when they leave nothing behind for me." She broke off the long kiss.

George smacked his lips. "They didn't eat me."

"They couldn't get near you, George boy. *You stunk.* You turned their stomachs, so they left you behind for me. But I can't eat you now, lover mine."

"I'm hungry right now," George announced, eyeing her. "And *you* look good enough to eat, baby."

"Now, George! You wouldn't like me and I wouldn't like you. You're still alive, George."

"I hope to tell you I'm still alive George!" George responded. He reached for the body. "Come to papa."

Why . . . you'd think he had dishonorable intentions.

It was long after midnight and the moon had vanished behind the opposite rim of the street canyon, leaving it in darkness. George Young lounged in the open doorway of a furniture store, scratching a stubble of beard on his face. The whiskey seemed to be wearing off, leaving him with a vaguely disappointed feeling. He turned his head to look at the blonde who was stretched out full length on a bed in the display window. She had vaguely disappointed him too, although he couldn't quite identify the cause of the dissatisfaction.

She raised her head and smiled. "Joyboy."

"I need a drink," he answered weakly.

The blonde leaped from the bed and worked her way through the articles in the window to join him. "I love rotgut!" she whispered, snuggling up to him.

"You and me both; I need a stiff one. All this talk about hunters and followers gives me the creeps."

"Oh, but they don't creep, George. I don't either."

He mumbled something under his breath and moved out to the curb. The girl came gliding after him. He stopped with one foot lifted from the curb to peer across the street, attempting to decipher a sign hanging in the darkness.

"What are you looking for, sweet man?"

"A drugstore. That one over there."

"What's a—Why?"

"To get a drink, quick." George stepped off the curb and crossed over, the girl still trailing after. The magic had somehow left her and he didn't bother to watch for the jiggles. The drugstore doors were closed but not locked, and he pushed in to look around. Bypassing the soda fountain and the candy counters, George made his way to the far side of the store and pawed over the displays until he found flashlights. He flicked a button and lit one.

"Ooooh, that's pretty, George."

Ignoring her, he followed the beam of light to the rear of the store and through a small white door marked PRIVATE. George found himself in the druggist's prescription and mixing room, surrounded by the ingredients of the trade. He flicked the light about the shelves.

"Bottles," the blonde squealed. "Look at all the nice rotgut!"

"Naw," George contradicted, "some of this stuff ain't fit to drink. Wait until I locate the good stuff."

The good stuff he searched for proved to be a gallon can of carbon tetrachloride, although he wasted the better part of half an hour finding it. Removing the lid, he took a quick sniff and tears formed in his eyes.

"Ahhh," he pronounced in satisfaction, "this is it. Doll, this'll send you."

"Will I like it, George?"

"Baby, you'll love it" He handed her the can and she nearly dropped it, not expecting the weight. "Bottoms up."

"What?"

"Wrap your mouth around that little spout and turn the can upside down. Best little old rotgut you ever tasted!" He stepped back to watch, playing the light on her.

She did as she was told, struggling to hold the heavy can over her head. The liquid made a gurgling noise as it poured from the spout. George waited, expectant.

"Wow!" she exclaimed after a moment and dropped the can. "Wow, George. People certainly make fine rotgut." Her eyes grew round and for a few seconds her head balanced precariously on her shoulders, wobbling from side to side. She put up her hands to steady it. "Why did we waste time in all those saloons?"

"I don't know," George said weakly. "I think I need a drink."

"Try some of mine, hotshot."

"No thanks—I've got ulcers." He turned the light on a display of bottles along the wall, and presently found several dark brown jars in a locked case. Smashing the door, he reached in for them and held the flash close to read the labels. *Strychnin*. He set it aside and turned his attention to the next bottle, *tincture of nux vomica*. The label puzzled him for a moment but he placed it beside the first bottle. In rapid succession he selected *acetanilid, aconite, cyanid, bichlorid of Mercury, sodium fluorid,* and *prussic acid*. His hand hesitated over *emetin* and then rejected it on the off chance it might be an emetic. George recognized only a few of the names but he was certain they were potent.

One by one he opened the bottles and dumped their contents into a mixing bowl. Poking around among the large jugs on a lower shelf, he discovered and added to the bowl a pint of methyl alcohol. The blonde obligingly held the light for him while he stirred the powders, dissolving them into the liquid.

"There!" George announced at last, peering into the deadly brew. He wondered if the little bubbles coming to the top would add zing. "I think I'll call it the Peoples' Cocktail." He took the light and handed the bowl to the girl. "Down the hatch."

"Bottoms up?"

"Bottoms up. And goodnight, babydoll."

She tilted the bowl to her lips and drained it. Then she sat down on the floor, hard. George turned the light on her. To his startled, wondering gaze her body seemed to scoot rapidly across the floor and smack against the far wall. The girl's head was completely turned about, facing the rear. An arm came loose at the shoulder and toppled to the floor. The blonde finally fell over. George walked over and played the light on her.

"Gee whiz," he said, quite shaken.

The head turned around again and her eyelids fluttered open. The beautiful golden eyes looked up at him, filled with adoration.

"Oh, George—you sweet man!"

He turned and ran for the street. In a moment he knew she was loping along behind him.

How he came to the bank and what caused him to turn in, George never afterward fully realized. He didn't put much stock in the manipulations of fate, and the guidings of the subconscious mind was but a meaningless phrase he had read somewhere. He was running along the darkened street in desperation, not unmixed with fright, when the gray marble building loomed up in the bobbing beam of the flashlight. He recognized the building as typical of banks everywhere, not actually dwelling on the thought, and turned to run through the double doors without hesitation. The blonde was hard on his heels.

Inside, he could think of nothing but to continue running. He darted through a swinging gate that marked off some manager's office, ran around behind a pair of desks and overturned chairs, and down the aisle behind the tellers' cages. At the far end of the big room the aisle opened onto another and smaller room filled with business machines, and just beyond that, George glimpsed a huge vault door resplendent in bronze and steel trim. He sped for the vault. The girl chased after him.

George dashed into the vault, flicked the light around wildly, and scooped up a brown canvas sack. The girl beside him snatched up its twin, and together they turned to run out again. George dropped his sack just outside the vault.

"Quick," he gasped, breathing hard from the effort, "money! Go get another one!"

She turned and reëntered the steel chamber. He slammed
the door on her, savagely twisting the spoked wheel that
secured it, just as savagely twirling the tumblers of the
combination locks. And then there was silence. George was
whistling as he left the bank.

Why . . . you'd think he had locked her away forever.

George Young critically examined his face in the mirror,
running a hand through his heavy beard and noting the
streaks of gray sprouting here and there. It would be turning soon, he decided, turning to match the shaggy gray at
his temples. He had long ago given up the task of shaving,
because shaving annoyed him and because there was no one
else to see him. Now, with a corner of his mind, he toyed
with the idea of removing the beard if only to remove those
irritating specks of gray from his daily inspection. He
didn't want to awaken some morning and have the mirror
tell him he was an old man, a graybeard. He preferred to
think of himself as a young man, as young as that whipper-
snapper who had climbed down off a train 30 years ago
and taken a whiskey shower, as young as the howling soldier who had owned a blonde and a town for one full night,
just once, 30 years ago.

George sighed and turned away from the mirror.

He picked up his carefully wrapped lunch, a book he
was slowly reading, and a tin of stale pipe tobacco. Leaving
the small cottage he had appropriated for himself, he
mounted a bicycle waiting at the bottom of the steps and
peddled off toward town, his legs dully aching with the advance of age. The sun was bright and warm on his bare
head and he took his time riding down to the bank. There
wasn't much of a breeze moving through the empty streets.

He liked to look at the familiar spots—here a saloon
where a bit of a swim suit still hung from a buck's antlers,
there a bed in a display window where he had briefly slept.
He never failed to pass the drugstore without recalling the
blonde's last words of endearment. The words and scenes
were all quite clear in his memory. Thirty years didn't seem
such a long time—until you began thinking of them in another way.

George parked the bicycle outside the bank and entered
the double doors, walking across a floor thick with money
because it pleased him to walk on it. Several years ago he
had scattered the money there, and had pulled a desk over

to the vault door, a desk now littered like a housekeeper's nightmare. The desk top was crammed with empty liquor bottles, old tobacco tins, books he had long since read, wadded papers from hundreds or thousands of past lunches, and mounds of pipe ashes. Over everything but the most recently used hung the dust of years. George cleared away a little space on a corner of the desk and put down his fresh lunch, his tobacco and the book he was reading that week. Finally he sat down in a comfortable chair and lit his pipe.

Hitching his chair up to the vault door, he scanned the endless possible combinations he had penciled there and noted those that had already been checked off. George took a heavy drink from the bottle, and leaned forward to put his hands on the tumblers, turning them. Any day now, or any year, he might hit upon the right combination.

Why . . . you'd think he wanted his blonde back again.

No one man or woman has managed to possess or rule the entire world since humans first appeared on earth. Of course, thousands have tried: kings and queens and generals and politicians, along with sergeants and corporals who believed their egos and ambitions were equal to the task. Ruling an entire world cannot be done with armies or scientific weapons or spell-binding oratory, but it might be accomplished by accident or a slip of the tongue. If you are a skeptic, an unbeliever, it might be accomplished by shooting off your mouth in the wrong place at the wrong time.

Kings as well as commoners are entitled to repent at leisure.

King of the Planet

KING OF THE PLANET

THE KING WAS ANNOYINGLY AWAKENED BEFORE dawn by a noise in the sky.

The noise was an ear-splitting roar, an avalanche of sound, a rushing, tumbling, thunderous reverberation which filled the heavens from one horizon to another, the kind of noise—and the volume—that might be expected on the day the sun cracked open. The shattering thunder shook the stout old building, causing the king of the planet to creep from his shabby bed and go to the window. The dawn was still an hour or more away.

Nothing but empty sky and the roseate flush in the east was visible from the tiny window, but yet the echoes of intruding sound lapped about the building. Blinking away sleep and muttering at the trespass, the king went to the door, circuitously avoiding the cracked marble urn in the exact center of the room which contained his drinking water. He stepped out into the high grasses surrounding the building and turned to look skyward. It was there, as he had guessed.

The source of the monstrous noise was a monstrous vehicle hanging many miles above him, as stationary as a rock, but even at that distance its enormous size was apparent. The thing hung effortlessly in the early morning sky, washed with the new sunlight, and seemed to be supported on small tongues of flame which everywhere studded its massive belly. A coruscating envelope of pale blue, much like ancient neon lighting, laved the vehicle to create an eerie illusion in the yellowish rays of the sun. The tremendous sound that had awakened him had been caused by the braking effort of the great machine.

The king studied it closely for many minutes, watching for a Sign—an Omen, searching for a sacred Token to suggest that it might be something other than what his mundane senses had taken it to be. He waited, but a Revelation did not come. There was nothing about the machine to excite his hopes.

It was only a starship.

It had disturbed his sleep and it was nothing more than a starship, probably inhabited by a pack of crazy fools bent on exploring each new planet to fall within their sights. Now they had discovered his, and in a few hours hordes of them would be descending on him.

The starship was too large and ungainly to land, but the people on it—if they were people—would come down on him like mosquitoes, in small scouting vessels, and conduct themselves like imbeciles on a picnic. Their military men would eye him suspiciously and cast dark glances at the surrounding forests. Their linguists would buzz about with primitive signs and symbols in an effort to establish communication. Their botanists would uproot great masses of weeds. Their archeologists would ransack the ruins and gouge deep holes in the ground, plundering graves, to carry away what they believed to be precious treasures, while their commander—ahh, the commander!

That nincompoop would fatuously plant a flag, or its gaudy equivalent, in the soil and claim ownership of the new world for his distant sovereign. The nincompoop would cheerfully ignore, of course, the very obvious fact that this world already possessed a sovereign.

A pox on them. Let them come down and play, and then go away again. They were not Significant. The starship had offered no Sign, and he was not greatly interested in its coming.

The king of the planet returned indoors and let himself down on the hard bed. He ruminated a short while and then drifted off to sleep, confident that their noisy scurryings would awaken him later.

He had momentarily considered closing the door, and then decided against it. The prying archeologists would probably come inside anyway; they would not be able to resist temptation, for the king's indigent residence was a marble mausoleum nearly hidden among the weeds and wild grasses of an incredibly ancient cemetery.

The king of the planet lived in a mausoleum because the structure had withstood the ravages of time, because he had made it somewhat comfortable, and because it had seemed the best place to wait.

A few minutes after sunrise, a single scout left the mother ship and landed almost directly beneath it, resting quietly—but watchfully—on a grassy clearing well away from the dense woods. More than half of the crew of twenty had emerged from the scout and fanned out, each crew member going about his particular business. Some of their number had already discovered a promising mound and were bringing up heavy equipment to probe its probable mystery. One man was taking samples of the vegetation, while another was trapping insects in the soil.

Within the small scout ship, a woman hunched over a set of scanning instruments, her head concealed in an enveloping hood, the better to watch a series of glass plates. She listened to a contact speaker fastened behind an ear and spoke into a throat microphone. There was a gentle excitement in her voice, but no trace of fear or hysteria.

"The life-form is approaching from the northwest. Movement slow but progress steady. Near you, Seven."

And a response from the clearing: "Seven, check."

The woman continued, dividing her attention between two devices: "It appears to be warm-blooded and intelligent. It does not show fear of us, nor does there seem to be curiosity. I see nothing to indicate a weapon; it is carrying something that might be a walking stick. Are you tracking, Seven?"

"Negative," Seven reported. "The trees interfere."

"Eight?" the woman asked next.

"Eight, negative," a new voice said. "I read nothing but soil life."

"There are birds in the far distance," she advised. "I expect our arrival has frightened them away. I have discovered no animal life except for—It has stopped." She scanned the disc attentively. "It has put down the walking stick. Now it is behind a tree. I am receiving only a small positive signal."

A deep male voice cut into the circuit. "Nineteen here," it said. "Your animal *is* intelligent. It put down the stick to avoid its being mistaken for a weapon, and now is likely peeping at us from behind a tree. I'll be right out with a translator." The male voice was exultant. "Gently, gentlemen, gently. We've found a prize!"

The woman at the scanner spoke up. "The object is moving—coming directly toward the vessel. Seven, it is almost upon you! Don't you see it?"

"Nega—*correction*." His voice jumped. "It's coming out now. I see it!"

"Eight, move in and cover," the woman snapped. "Two, start recording."

"I'm forty-five seconds ahead of you," Two replied dryly. "Sight, sound and depth."

"Be careful!" Nineteen cried, "Don't scare it away. What is it—what does it look like?"

The communication channel was silent for a moment and then Seven said, "It looks like you. It's a *man*."

"Are you certain?" the woman demanded.

"It's a man," the dry voice of the recorder cut in. "I can tell by his innards."

Seven reported: "An old man; quite aged by the looks of him. Extremely long hair and long beard. He is naked—I think. And he needs a bath."

"Weapons?"

"Negative, unless there is one hidden under the beard. *There*—he's out of the woods. See him?"

"I see him," she answered, and stared for a long moment. "I wish I could be more impressed. Well, I suppose we must extend the customary welcome. He is the only life-form—" he corrected herself—"the only human to reveal sign on this planet. Stand by, Seven."

The king of the planet left the shadow of the trees and made his careful way into the clearing. He moved slowly because he could not trust his limbs to any reasonable speed and because he did not want to frighten the visitors into an unfriendly act. He had no wish to be a cripple after their departure.

The king paused ten or twelve feet short of the nearest intruder and examined the ship. His examination was a cursory one because he was little interested in its origin, its means of locomotion, or its physical properties. There had been others like it and unlike it, and doubtless there were more to come. The ship and the travelers were merely transients.

The impudent young fellow a dozen feet away stared at him with a friendly, idiotic grin. His feet were braced wide apart, his hands were outstretched—palms upward—

in the usual gesture of welcome, and not too far away his mate waited with one hand resting on the butt of a weapon. They were military men, making their customary two-faced show of welcome.

The king looked at the friendly face and the grinning lips and wanted to snarl, looked at the upturned palms and wanted to spit on them, but he realized that such behavior would only complicate matters. It was better to help them tidy up their business and send them on their way.

He stuck out his two hands in an imitative gesture and tried to smile. It didn't quite come off.

"Now that's done," he grunted. "Get on with your picking and clear off my planet!"

Seven did not understand him, of course, and promptly launched into a lengthy torrent of unintelligible speech which was the Response Courteous, the standard rejoinder to a native welcome.

The Response Courteous was grandiose, pompous and rhetorical, punctuated with graceful gestures and primitive symbolisms; the eloquent sentry called upon the local rain god to increase the old man's crops and upon the sun god to bless his aged bones; he complimented the native on his health, wealth and appearance, thanked him for so graciously offering the hospitality of his planet, begged him to allow them to stay a few days more that they might explore and catalogue the new world, flattered him with the observation that no other mud ball in the Universe was so beautiful as this one, assured him that they would do harm to none, and ended—finally—by respectfully inquiring after the old one's lovely wife (wives?) and sturdy children.

It was an impressive speech, recited letter-perfect from the field manual.

The sentry then bowed and mumbled an aside into his microphone. "I don't think I want to meet his lovely wife. I wish I was upwind of him."

Two, the dry commentator operating the recording machine, suggested: "Perhaps you'd better run through that again. Nothing stirred beneath the leathery hide."

"I'll make you a wager," Seven retorted. "I don't believe he *has* a rain god."

"Patience, gentlemen—I'm coming." Nineteen came running from the lock of the scout ship. He carried a large bronze box which contained his own specialized exploring tool, and he was wearing a large, pleased smile. Behind him ran a pretty, youthful girl carrying two pillows.

The newcomers slowed cautiously as they approached the king of the planet and set down their equipment for his inspection. The king ignored Nineteen and his box to stare at the girl and her pillows.

She dropped to her knees, placed a pillow on the ground behind him, and invited him to sit. The king sat, staring at the girl's bosom and bare legs. She smiled winningly and moved over to place a pillow for her superior. Nineteen seated himself and opened the lid of the bronze box. It contained an array of instruments and two slim bronze cables which terminated in handgrips.

Nineteen placed a microphone on the ground between himself and the native, switched on his apparatus and motioned to the assistant. The girl removed the coiled cables from their nest and gave one to the old man, showing him how to hold the grooved handle with his curled fingers. The other cable was given to the smiling translator. An electrical connection was completed between the two men, monitored by the translating rig.

"H-2 type," Nineteen murmured into his throat microphone.

"H-2 *sub-a*," the distant recorder corrected him matter-of-factly. "Plus *sub*-something else which I am not qualified to identify. I recognize only a vague x quality to his digestive and regenerative systems."

"Beetles and birchbark," was Seven's snide reply.

"Perhaps, but I daresay Hundred-Ten would like to lay him on her surgical table upstairs. He'd make a splendid subject for study."

Nineteen cleared his throat meaningfully and the communication circuit went silent. He smiled again at the dour old man who was eyeing the girl.

"How do you do, sir?"

The king of the planet stared down at the handgrip in his gnarled fingers and wondered how they'd managed that trick; he had both heard and *felt* the smiling idiot's words, and the utilization of the two senses enabled him to grasp the meaning of the question. It also caused him to realize they would understand his replies only too well, unless he was careful.

(The recorder whispered: "Curiosity, and mental reservations.")

("I expected it," Nineteen replied.) To the old one, he said, "I am Nineteen, a linguist. Who are you?"

No harm in answering that. "I am the king of the planet."

Nineteen watched the analyzers in the bronze box. (His communicator whispered: "Truth, pride.") "What are you called, sir?"

The king grunted. "Many things. Ahasuerus, Joseph, Isaac, Salatheil ben Sadi . . . I am called many names."

(The whisper: "Bitterness.")

Nineteen correctly deduced that the old one had referred to himself as the leader, or overlord, of the entire world; but the multiplicity of names confused him and he was not certain that he could pronounce any of them accurately.

"Jo-seff," he said, and watched to see if the native took offense at a possible mispronunciation. "The leader of the world. Where are your people, Jo-seff?"

"The damned fools are dead," the king retorted. "Every one of them."

"They have expired? *All* of them?"

"That's what I said."

"How did they die, Jo-seff? Why did they die?"

"Because they were damned fools."

("Vituperation, anger, vague hatred.")

Nineteen repeated gently, "How did they die? What caused *all* their deaths, Jo-seff?"

"Peace!" the king spat. "Eternal peace. Senility, sterility, boredom, retrogression. They curled up in their chosen wombs and died."

"I don't understand, Jo-seff."

"That's too bad." The king abruptly switched languages because it pleased him to do so and because his interrogator was becoming too inquisitive. He lapsed into Latin, a tongue barely remembered. "They abolished conflict and returned to Paradise. *That* was the end of them."

(Two reported: "Evasive tactics, but still truth.")

Nineteen frowned and realized something was amiss. He studied his analyzers but found nothing wrong there; they continued to monitor and report the speech patterns in the normal fashion, giving normal readings, but despite that, he recognized a change in routine. The ancient king's subjects had stopped fighting among themselves and perished as a result—that much was clear. But the exact manner of their going and the last two sentences were puzzling.

("Is this doubletalk?" he asked the recorder.)

("No, sir. Clear and straightforward.")

"They died suffering peace, Jo-seff?"

"They did."

"How can this be?"

"Easier than you think."

"You did not die with them?" Nineteen asked tactfully. The king glowered, considering the question silly.

Nineteen rephrased the question. "Can you tell me, sir, why you did not suffer this same death?"

"I refused peace."

"It was a matter of acceptance or rejection?"

"It was."

"You are the only living human in all this world?"

"I am."

"I do not understand how they *all* suffered and died of this peace simultaneously."

"I didn't say that!" the king snapped. "Idiot." He searched among the languages familiar to him and said, "Degeneration. Dry rot requires only a few centuries.

Again the interpreter noted a subtle but baffling difference to the response. As before, the old man's answer was partly understood and partly guessed at, and, as before, the analyzing equipment performed in normal fashion, but for the second time there had been an undefined *change* in the procedure. "Degeneration" and "dry rot" were undoubtedly a form of slow death; while "centuries" was probably one or more measurable units of time.

"I ask your pardon, great leader," Nineteen continued smoothly. "I believe I now understand. Your subjects suffered peace for a number of centuries and gradually perished; a kind of lingering death. Is that correct?"

The king of the planet nodded dourly, his attentive eyes following the lithe movements of the young girl as she fidgeted in the grass.

"Thank you, sir. And what is a *century?*"

"One hundred years."

"Ah, yes. And what constitutes a *year*, sir?"

"One revolution about the sun!" The king looked at his questioner with scorn. "Is a star-traveler ignorant of the most basic astronomy?"

Nineteen jumped with astonishment and listened to the murmur of surprise on the communication circuit. "Ah— then you *are* aware of our identity?"

The king was disgusted. "I know a starship when I see one, you fool!"

"Your great wisdom pleases me, honorable leader. Have *other* starships visited your kingdom?"

"Of course. How else would I know, stupid?"

(The woman at the scanning plates said excitedly: "There are no records of any known ship visiting this planet.")

(The recording engineer said: "Nonetheless, he's telling the truth. And he thinks us a pack of fools.")

("Most amazing," Nineteen commented. "And perhaps we are—he certainly was not excited to see us, remember. Evidently his memory antedates our records. Let's put the prime question.")

Nineteen returned his attention to the native. "August leader, you must have lived a very long time to have watched your people perish over the centuries, and to have seen the visiting starships. Good sir, what is the number of your glorious years?"

Bitterly, the king of the planet told him.

The answer was not immediately intelligible, for it involved still another x unit of local time, and, to compound matters, there had been still another shift of tonal values. Grimly, not unmixed with annoyance, the king once more changed languages and answered the question—quite honestly—in Moabitish.

His questioner could only determine that the old man's unusual life span had stretched over an x number of centuries, and he had to be content with that for the time being. But the interrogation continued.

For the remainder of that day, and the following three, the space visitors posed endless questions. They were insatiable.

Nineteen, prompted by whispers from within the ship, from those waiting far above, and from the technicians working about the clearing, valiantly attempted to pump the king of his knowledge of anthropology, archaeology, astronomy, architecture, biology (running from botany through zoology—although biometrics proved to be a most frustrating business), chemistry, commerce, electronics, geology and geography, history (a fruitful mass of data!), mathematics, medicine and pharmacy, mythology, numeration—the list of subjects and the many detailed questions pertinent to each appeared to have no end.

The visitors pried and the old man answered in his fashion. He darted from one subfamily of languages to another, leaping from tongue to dialect and back again, watching the interpreter with malicious amusement. Without warning, he would turn from ultra-modern English to Prakrit, to Illyrian, to French, to Avestan, to Vulgate Latin, to Chaldean, to Pahlavi and then to Umbrian, always secretly amused in the belief that he was bewildering the inquisitor. His mastery of the many languages was as complete as his aged memory would permit and he was enjoying himself— until he suddenly discovered that the space visitor was wise to his game.

At some time during the lengthy sessions, the visitor had discovered the subterfuge and thereafter ignored the dazzling changes. The king of the planet lapsed into Aramic, his favorite tongue, and remained there. The malicious fun was lost.

The sessions were not continuous. They paused many times to rest because the king tired, and because he would fall into moody silences that could not be broken until he was ready to break them. They stopped then to eat and drink, and the young girl would bring food from the ship and place it before the old one.

He ate sparingly.

They took the time to inspect the many small discoveries the archeologists were bringing back from the ancient cemetery, and at the close of each day they closed up shop to sleep. The king refused the invitation to sleep in the scout, or in the mother ship hanging far above, always preferring to return to his mausoleum.

Before the king quit the clearing at the end of the first day, he made a small request, a mild one which surely could offend nobody, but it had to be refused. The translator was very sorry, but he simply could not permit the young girl to accompany the king back to his bed for the night. It just wasn't done, and besides the girl was under age. Respectful regret and all that.

The king strode away, greatly irritated.

On the morning of the second day, the king was awakened by the noise the archeologists were making in the mausoleum, and he chased them outdoors. He let them know with strong language and unmistakable gestures that his home was the one sacred place barred to them. They could *not* knock holes in the many vaults lining the mausoleum walls—not even the small holes which would admit their camera lenses.

On the morning of the third day, the visitors had charted the local time sequences to their satisfaction, and the new-found knowledge excited them.

Nineteen probed for a solution to the riddle.

"Great sir, did many of your people live through centuries? That is, for many hundreds of years?"

"No."

"What was their usual lifetime?"

"The good died young—they knew better than to stay alive. The worthless ones stayed longer; they were too mean to die."

"But what number of years, great leader?" Nineteen strove for the impression of worshipping at the old man's hardened feet. "How young is young?"

"Thirty or forty years," the king said impatiently.

"And how old is old?"

"Seventy, eighty, ninety. A few lived past the century."

"Ah, yes. But that extreme age was a rarity, was it not? Even when your subjects were not suffering peace?"

"Of course."

"Pardon me, glorious one, but I do not understand your age. Why is it that you live so long?"

"I rejected peace—I've told you that!"

"You did, good sir, but we still do not understand. Is not peace a desirable attainment?"

"It is, until you get it. And then you rot."

"And you rejected peace and thus avoided rotting. I'm afraid that isn't as simple as it sounds, but then I do not expect to understand the theory. But, sir, there must be some *rational* reason for your tremendous age, some *fact* that you have not made known to us."

The king stared at him, unwilling to answer.

"Have you discovered the secret of eternal life?" Nineteen asked anxiously. "Do you take drugs? Is it a dietary matter? Have you found some unknown substance which prolongs your life?"

The king let his attention wander and fastened his gaze on the young girl, who was helping a botanist.

("Keep at it," the recording engineer whispered. "You scored a clean hit with one of those questions. His pulse raced.")

"My own life," Nineteen said smoothly, "and the lives of my companions are reasonably long. We may expect to live about two hundred years, if we are fortunate."

The king pointed at the girl. "How old is she?"

"Not yet forty." Nineteen smiled. "She is my daughter, an apprentice to this crew." Without changing his conversaional tone, he asked, "How old are you?"

The king replied with the identical answer given on the first day.

"But sir!" the translator declared. "That amounts to more than three thousand years! And that is incredible; I can scarcely believe it. How does one live for three thousand years by simply rejecting peace?"

"It depends upon the manner of rejection," the old one said dourly. "And the time, and the place, and the catalyst." His hungering gaze would not leave the girl.

"I'm afraid I do not understand you at all."

"I didn't expect you to."

"It just isn't possible to exist for so long!"

"I'm existing." The king raised his eyes to the scout ship. "And that fellow yonder knows I'm not lying."

(The whisper: "He isn't lying, but you've hit on something. I believe he is superstitious. Question him.")

Nineteen did, digging patiently but as deeply as he was able, utilizing his every skill to draw out the old man. He reverted to a subject they had discussed on a previous day, mythology, and examined it more carefully than before.

A number of significant things came to light which had been passed over before, and these new factors were weighed and balanced against all the conversations so far recorded.

In the end, Nineteen admitted to a partial defeat. The day drew to a close and he packed away his equipment, preparatory to returning to the mother ship; he wished he

could remain a month or a year with the aged native, but
that was not possible. They were leaving after darkness fell.

Lugging their gear and their specimens, their recordings
and their artifacts, the explorers returned to the scout. The
military men dismantled the tall pole which had been
planted in the clearing, and reverently packed away the
varicolored ball that had spun atop it.

Food and drink were left outside, as a final tribute to
the king of the planet, and the scout was made secure for
lifting.

"It is imperative that we return to this planet," Nineteen
declared later. "Perhaps in a century or two. It is important
to know if he will still be living."

"He will be," Seven predicted lightly. "Beetles and birchbark will keep going forever."

"Not forever," Nineteen contradicted, ignoring the levity.
"Even he admitted it. But that last session was most pro-
ductive; it *must* have high priority in translation and anal-
ysis. I wish I understood it more clearly now. No—he won't
live forever. He is aware of his eventual death, and, if my
intuition is correct, he is looking forward to it. Can you
imagine three thousand years?"

"I can't," Seven replied.

"Nor I, but I expect we will find he is very much correct
in the figure. No wonder he wants release! His future death
is hopelessly entangled in some supernatural fantasy; I no
more understand *that* than I understand his fantastic reason
for longevity. What is myth and what is real?"

Two said, "He believes in those old gods of the myth, believes in them flatly and without question. Do you suppose
there is something to mythology after all?"

Nineteen smiled and shrugged. "I'm too old to say *nonsense,* however much I am tempted. But how many hundreds of fantastic legends have we stumbled over? How
many wild fictions of imaginary men and imaginary monsters? They persist even in civilized areas. This one appears
to be simply another variation—except that *this* one is
living."

Seven laughed. "Yes—in a cemetery."

"He explained that. Again the explanation is caught up
in myth. His god, or gods, are supposed to revisit the planet
some day and take up all the spirits; when they left thousands of years ago, they promised they would come a

second time. This second visitation is supposed to be a universal reawakening day, and the old leader sleeps in the midst of the dead so that he will not be overlooked when that day comes. It is the release he is expecting."

"Release from eternal life? That is a favor?"

Two cut in dryly, "Try it sometime."

"I might, if I get the chance," Seven agreed. "How did the old boy manage it?"

"I don't know how it really happened," Nineteen said. "But according to his mythology, he angered the gods by rejecting peace and was sentenced to live until they came again. The gods won't permit his death until that day. I wish I could get to the *truth* of the matter!"

The king of the planet heard the starship go. It quit the sky with a repetition of the thunder which had accompanied its arrival, and after its passing the world was strangely quiet.

It was always like that after a big ship had passed, but presently the night sounds would return and the lonely world would be normal again. In a century or so, or perhaps three, or five, another ship would come and more visitors would descend on him, annoying him, questioning him, taunting him.

Without realizing it, they always taunted him.

For none of them was the one visitor he awaited.

To be sentenced to prison is a shattering experience, but it is worse to serve that sentence among a thousand other prisoners as wretched and as desperate as you are. To escape prison is an exhilarating experience, and never mind the extra years that are added to a sentence if the escapee is caught and returned. Don't be caught. Don't be found out years later and returned. Be more intelligent than the common culprit and seek a never-before-tried method of escaping the cell. Make sure the escape is planned all the way through. Your name will be written in the criminal history books.

EXIT

His was Cell One.

He was a small, dark-skinned Italian and he kept muttering *"Hell!"* aloud, over and over in droning monotony. He seemed not to understand that at long last his particular fate had tagged him, was right now tagging at his heels. He didn't seem to realize that he had but one more week of life; that this was his last mile.

He said only, "Hell!"

The corridor was short, dank, brilliantly lighted. A guard stood at either end motionless but alert. A third sat in the center of the corridor, facing the cells. Drab, cement-block walls were painted a chalky white, a deathly white. Damp drafts scudded constantly across the scoured floor, climbing the sticky wall at the far end of the corridor; crept silently across a cold metal door embedded there. A dark green door having a black knob. The last door.

The draft drifted back across the room, waist-high. "Hell!"

The clerk was in Cell Two.

An ordinary appearing clerk; he would have been an unseen fixture in any office. He sat dejectedly on a white metal bunk, weeping, pale with the thought of the thing to come; his pallor matched that of the cheerless walls about him. He wept continuously.

He had been crying for three unending weeks. His swollen eyes no longer welled tears but he cried on—a dry, disturbing cry. He would cry for one week more.

Set in the dull white ceiling a glassy brilliant eye, as bright as a carbon arc, burned relentlessly. It was never turned off. The probing rays burned into the eyelids of the men when they tried to sleep, burned into the muddy conscious when they lay there simply staring and thinking—or not thinking. It burned into their minds when they cried for peace, for darkness, for that which could not be

94

found. The blinding light illuminated every corner, every inch of the corridor and the four white cells.

It brought out in bold relief each bunk and each occupant, it dispelled any shadows that may have lurked behind the white-painted bars. It burned.

"Hell!"

Cell Three held a huge and bulky body.

An overgrown ape of a man, unmoving and silent. Two great hamlike hands supported an equally massive head; his skin was coarse and matted with hair, spikelike whiskers jutted out all over the clipped, bullet chin. Eyes were yellowish with hate, eyes narrow and unblinking but slitted against the blinding light. Eyes that stared with undying hatred at the brass-buttoned, blue uniform stationed in the center of the corridor—just safely out of reach.

The occupant of Cell Three would go to his death a week hence—hating, silent, contemptuous.

The guard sitting in the center of the corridor was colorless, quiet, and but for a slow, measured mastication of chewing gum, almost unmoving. Gleaming brass buttons marched in two orderly rows down the breast of his uniform, rows now twisted slightly out of line because he slouched in his chair. He never for an instant moved his eyes from the activities or non-activities of the four imprisoned men before him, never permitted a breath or a batted eye to go unnoticed. Set in the dank cement floor near his foot was the alarm button.

The guard at either end of the corridor watched him. The three of them, the three men keeping the death watch on four, were changed every two hours. This was the death row, this was Joliet.

"Hell!"

The man in Cell Four read a book.

He seemed not to be disturbed by the mutterings of the Italian, the clerk's incessant weeping, nor was he disturbed by the ominous and brooding silence in the cell next to his. He was absorbed by the book. The book should be finished and then dwelt upon before he was forced to put it down forever.

Forever was coming soon: midnight, tonight.

The book was all that was important; it would be a great pity were he to die before gaining a few more items of knowledge the book might contain for him. He considered not at all the fact that additional knowledge would be useless to him beyond midnight, tonight. He turned the pages rapidly, reading thoroughly.

The bars were white, like the ceiling, like the floor, like the walls. The iron bunk fastened securely and solidly to a white wall. A white, canvas-covered ticking covered each bunk; each man wore a pair of white canvas trousers, a pair of soft slippers. The chest was bare. And continually that chilling draft swung across the floor to gather more dampness and drift back, waist-high, across the light-etched room.

In a week's time three of them would die: the Italian, who slew his wife and four children; the clerk, who murdered his sweetheart when he found her pregnant; the hulking ape, who bashed together the skulls of two policemen. The three of them would go trooping through the dark green door in ghastly parade. The man with the book had only the remainder of the day; he had killed his wife, he claimed with a soft smile, because she talked too much.

"Hell!"

A gong clanged somewhere far away. Meal time. After an interval the door opened and the odor of cooked food seeped in, brushing before it the dingy smell of prison disinfectant. The Italian glanced up at the noise, at the movement of the door and let the unspoken word die on his lips. Food was understood if death was not. Next to him the clerk peered hopefully from between the bars, his sobs forgotten for the moment. It would be the usual deep pan of soup, or meat stew, or meat loaf, that and a hunk of bread and black coffee—but it was something to eat and do and it shattered the monotony of nothingness.

The hairy one said nothing, moved nothing but his eyes; they shifted toward the door where another uniform had appeared carrying a tray. He waited stolidly.

The man in Cell Four laid down his book almost regretfully. His tray was brought in first. He sat without smiling on the edge of his bunk as the guard entered the cell and placed the tray on the floor. The guard then took up a position against the cell door, inside, watching the man eat. The door was locked behind him.

Traditional last meal. There was a half chicken, which had not been requested. The reader pushed the book away and put the tray on the bunk. He sat beside it to eat.

"Good reading, prof?"

"Yes, yes indeed." The scholarly eyes glanced up at the waiting guard, friendly and intelligent. "A book you know is man's best friend—not the dog." He ate slowly. "My only regret is that I shall not have time to finish this one; it is so completely absorbing. I had hoped, you know, to work completely through your excellent library here, but——"

"Sure, I know. Tough luck, prof." The sympathy seemed not quite genuine.

"Not *professor*," the prisoner attempted to correct, "but . . . oh, never mind. I only wish I could finish it."

The waiting guard shrugged. "Every man to his own taste, I always say. I'd rather eat, myself. And I can think of a lot of things I'd sooner call a friend than that. Besides, what's so hot about this one?"

He reached out a casual hand to turn the book over on the bunk, reading the title: *Atoms and Their Properties*. "Oh, that stuff."

"Yes, that stuff." The twinkling eyes glanced up from the tray to smile guilelessly. "In that book sir, one finds an excellent means of escape. *If* one could but take advantage of it."

At the word *escape* all activity ceased.

The other guards swung around to stare with suspicion, their bodies alert. Eyes in the neighboring cubicles turned in unison toward Cell Four. Silence.

"What?" The guard within the cell shot out a quick hand to grab the volume. "Let me see that!" His companions outside in the corridor had approached the cell.

"What book is that?"

The title was read aloud. They stared at the scholarly man for the space of several seconds. The guard within the cell eyed him in speculative wonder; he wished he had paid more attention to high school physics. Atoms, now? Those unseen little things that whirl around inside a man, inside all objects, inside everything—that's what atoms were. But escape? Ridiculous!

He said as much, after thumbing the pages.

"And I agree with you, sir." The prisoner's eyes were still laughing. "But possible, nevertheless. And it has occurred before, I do suspect. But please do not let it worry you so!" His face was innocent and appeared totally incapable of plotting and executing any kind of escape.

"I don't know, prof——Maybe you'd better not read this book any more."

"Oh, please. I already have all the information necessary for such a step, I assure you—although it isn't likely that I can put it to good use. But I should like to finish the book before . . . well, I dearly want to finish it."

The guard was a picture of indecision. "No, I don't know about this." A last request was a last request and usually honored as such—within reason. On the other hand suppose there was something in this book? Damn atoms and physics! What to do?

"Oh, hell. Just what's in this book? Plenty of guys read it before you did and they didn't escape."

"That, sir"—and the white teeth showed quickly, "is probably because they weren't fortunate enough to take advantage of the phenomena. For that matter, neither am I. The laws of chance seldom work in one's favor."

"Listen, prof, if you want this book back you'd better come clean. Cut out that nonsense—otherwise, back to the office it goes." The guard was turning sour, his patience at an end. He couldn't decide whether atoms were in physics or astronomy and it annoyed him. "Spill it now, what's this all about?"

The scholar seated himself on the bunk, crossed his legs and patted his mouth with a paper napkin. The last meal was over.

He said, "I gather that you have never read that book, my friend. Also that you are probably not familiar with the properties and behavior patterns of the atom." His smile was most disarming.

"I ain't got time to read books, prof. A man hardly has time to read a newspaper around here."

"But really, you *should* take time to peruse this one. A highly instructive volume, really. Though your time may be limited I do not doubt but that you would be amply rewarded. But now, to answer you in brief: when, in flight of theoretical fancy, the laws of chance co-operate with the atomic structure of two physical bodies, those two bodies may perform astounding feats of legerdemain. That is, an explosion may occur, or one may walk through a steel door, or a wall, or even sink through the floor—all unharmed."

The guard stared at him thunderstruck, his jaw hanging slack in abrupt amazement. Suddenly recovering, he burst out laughing and tossed the book onto the bunk.

"Okay, prof, you can keep it! You sure had me going

there, I don't mind telling you." Genuine amusement shook his body. "Oh, brother! Call me, will you prof, when you get ready to do your fade-away? I want to be around to see that." He reached for the tray. "Through the floor yet!" The cell door was unlocked and the guard was let out; he went up the corridor laughing. In the death row on the third floor of the old Joliet prison his was not the only laughter.

"Shut up you bastards!"

For the first time in weeks the huge ape spoke. His hamlike hands dropped from propping up his head and he turned his strange, unwavering eyes on the neighboring cell. He seemed to discover the mild little man there for the first time. His gaze was brimming with curiosity, aroused interest. He said, "I like you, Doc."

"Thank you."

"Yeah, I like you." Calculating eyes set in the massive head roamed over the scholar's small body. "You're okay. You ain't bats like these other birds—you gotta good head." His eyes glanced once at the book. "Sure, I like you."

"Thank you. And may I add that I harbor no ill feelings toward you?"

"Yeah, I suppose so. We understand each other, huh?" He hunched forward and pointed an oversize finger. "Is that the truth, Doc? About what you said to brass buttons? Can a guy just get up and change his atoms and walk through that wall?"

His intended whisper resembled a muted roar. The clerk looked around at him, his attention caught. In the far cell the dark-skinned man uttered a single, contemptuous, "Hell!" and turned his back. The three guards looked on, half interested, half amused.

"Why, yes, it *is* theoretically true, I suppose, but not in the literal sense you imply. Actually, it is very much open to question. There is a school of belief which holds that it has happened; history has recorded such incidents. Well-known personages *have* vanished from jail cells and asylums, from rooms supposed to be escape-proof. When the door was opened, *poof*—they were gone. And sometimes they bobbed up elsewhere in the world.

"But understand this, it is—well, practically impossible. I say it is theoretically possible only because past incidents suggest it has happened. Not everyone can expect to do it, not in the longest lifetime imaginable. It could only happen once in so many hundreds of millions of times. Perhaps a bare half dozen occurrences from the day of Creation unto the end of time itself."

Unexpectedly the clerk spoke. "I haven't read anything about it happening."

"Of course not, sir. You will very seldom find such things recorded elsewhere than in prisons or asylums, and then you may be sure the news wouldn't be published. And who would bother to set down an abstraction at a time of hue and cry for an escaped prisoner? Perhaps in the long run the fellow was termed a magician, a partner of the devil, and eventually forgotten. But I believe it has happened."

"Doc—do you mean that if a hundred million other guys was in this cell with me, one of them could walk right out through that wall?" The gross face was deeply interested despite the skepticism he chose to display. Beyond him, the clerk clung to a horizontal bar of the cell, watching and listening.

"Oh, no, hardly that." The question seemed to amuse the scholar. "What I meant to imply was, given an unlimited number of years in which to live, and given the energy to go on forever without pause, a man could, *eventually,* walk through a solid wall or some similar object. In some one of his attempts, in a million-million attempts, he could and would succeed. It might occur on the tenth try, or the thousand and tenth, or it well might be the hundred million and tenth.

"Those who have escaped by such a method, if indeed they did escape that way and were not smuggled out, were fortunate enough to discover the laws of chance suddenly working in their favor. And in all probability, absolutely unknown to them. I would hazard a guess that they were merely leaning against the wall of their prison, or perhaps stamping the floor in rage—when miraculously they sank through. I doubt too that they realized afterward what happened to them."

"A miracle, huh?"

"They might attribute it to a miracle, or perhaps a weak wall, or simply that they had become insane."

"Hell!" the man in Cell One responded.

"Shaddup you rat!" The big fellow wished the Doc

hadn't used so many big words. The idea was slowly but painfully growing clear to him.

The clerk seemed to grasp the idea at once. "Then at almost any time, professor, a man can pass through an object, providing the laws of chance have arranged his atoms so that they don't collide?" He had forgotten to resume his crying.

"That's about as simple a way to state it, yes. And it is correct enough for us to speculate upon here. But I must caution you, do not expect the event to work for you as you would a wheel of fortune in a gaming house. Making a fortune upon a turn of the wheel is child's play in comparison; the odds are many times reduced."

"Hell," said the Italian. "I t'ink you crazy."

"That is quite possible, sir."

"I told you to shaddup, you rat!" The bellowing roar shook the walls and seemed to cause the white bars to rattle in their sockets. The Italian retreated to the far corner of his cell and flung back a weak, defiant, "Hell!"

"Go on, Doc. How does this business work?" The disbelief on the grizzled face was slowly fading, and something resembling a limited understanding was taking its place. "Go on, tell me."

"Atoms are—" the keen eyes surveyed the heavy face hanging beyond the bars "—atoms are small particles inside your body that cannot be seen or felt. But they are there, many millions of them, making up the entire bulk of your body or any physical object. Uncounted millions of them are constantly revolving about, inside you; were there no atoms there would be no you. When your body dies they cease operating, become something else—dust perhaps, and you no longer exist. They cease moving in their orbits and transmigrate to some other form."

"Like them germs, huh?" A grunt accompanied the question as if the entire matter was now fully understood.

"If that helps you understand the better, yes. But much smaller remember, because atoms exist even inside the germs. Billions of atoms within your finger alone."

The great head swung down to stare at his fingers in surprise. Experimentally he pushed a finger against the wall. "It didn't go through, Doc."

"Of course not. You surely don't expect to accomplish anything on the first try. The laws of chance would have to be operating very well indeed for such quick success.

And too, if it *had* worked that one time, it might have become stuck in the wall. There is no guarantee that an object will pass completely through another without collision.

"It might you see, and again it might not. There is a strong possibility that it would pass into a wall but still not be able to emerge from the opposite side. In which event, you are imprisoned within the wall." The pleasant smile disappeared. "Which would not be very nice, I assure you."

Undaunted, the big man sat on his bunk, pushing his finger again and again at the wall until a red welt appeared on the skin. One or two of the guards were listening and watching. The clerk joined the conversation.

"Do you mind explaining that, professor? The atom part, I mean . . . walking through the wall but not coming out the other side."

"Simple, sir. Every object on earth—the planet itself—is made up of atoms that are, quite naturally, revolving at tremendous speeds. Now let us suppose that the atoms of one's body suddenly find themselves (and this is where the laws of chance permit the impossible) on the same plane of rotation as the atoms of the wall, let us say. Not only on an identical plane of rotation, but rotating in such a manner as to permit the two types to slide between each other without touching—without collision. Think of a bag of marbles in your hand, constantly moving about and exchanging places with one another, but without actually making contact.

"This would permit one, if he happened to be leaning against the wall, to—uh, float, seemingly, through the wall but not actually touch it. When these two atoms slip between one another without collision, then two bodies may occupy the same space at the same time. It is when they refuse to slip and slide freely between each other, but constantly repel, that your body is rebuffed by the wall. In fact, that a wall stands at all."

The gangster's face suddenly lit up. "I got it, Doc! I got it."

"Yes?"

"Yeah—sure. You mean like the moon slides between the earth and the sun, but don't hit neither of them. Don't you, Doc?" The author of that profound statement was beaming with pride.

A mere whisper, "Hell!"

*   *   *

The few gentlemen of the press who came up from the city papers sat around the dismal press room with their coat collars turned up, their hats on. Turned up against the chill of the wind and rain outside, against the smell of death and disinfectant inside.

It was past eleven-thirty; at a quarter to twelve they would file solemnly and self-consciously into a small room to sit on ill-fitting benches and watch a man die for the murder of his wife. Afterwards they would return to town, would stop at the first available place to wash down with whiskey the sight and smell of death.

At a quarter to twelve a buzzer sounded in the press room, summoning them to the electrocution chamber. No one heard the buzzer.

Instead, the interior of the building was filled with a brazen clanging that drowned out all other sound, froze all movement, silenced all words, while outside atop the water tower a siren cried in the wet night air. The bell and siren caused the skin to crawl at the nape of the neck. They carried an insistent, sinister appeal.

In the warden's office a number flashed on the electric control board, a number locating the source of the trouble, a number when combined with the bell and the siren told of the impossible. Escape from the death row.

The floor was white, like the ceiling, like the walls, like the bars of each cell. In the spotless white ceiling the miniature sun burned on, revealing each detail, forbidding shadows. The damp draft swept across the floor, swept across the body of the guard who lay beside the alarm bell; the draft climbed the far wall and drifted back waist high through the cells. The eyes of the dead guard bulged in their sockets, the face an almost readable mask of terror, of insane shock, apoplectic death.

Cell One held a dazed Italian who stared at nothing, who pointed a finger at nothing. "Hell!" Sweat beaded his naked chest and ran down his stomach. "Hell!"

In Cell Two a thin, gaunt, crazed shadow of a man hurled his broken body again and again at the stolidly resisting wall. His eyes were filled with blood and his head was becoming a pulpy mass of featureless flesh. Time and again he threw his body at the resisting wall, heeding not the broken rib driving deep into a punctured lung with each mad thrust.

The overgrown man in Cell Three sat on the floor. He

stared with hatred at the dead guard just out of reach. "I counted them," he said to the body. "Doc did pretty good. I counted them. I know."

Cell Four was empty.

Outside the building a group of guards had gathered in the courtyard; a newspaper man or two ran across the paved area to join them, to stare at what they were staring at. The wet and silent mob of men huddled at the base of the building.

The scientific experimenter had successfully cleared the cell wall—without "collision." But it had been a three-story drop to the courtyard below.

The prevalence of ghosts is historically documented; they have appeared as well in the fields of anthropology and archaeology so there must be more to them than wisps of frightened imagination. Consider an indistinct, gauzy, semi-transparent figure of a nude male seen in a wall painting of a townhouse in ancient Jericho: Is it but the fading remnant of a much earlier picture bleeding through into and onto the new mural, or is it the delineation of a ghost seen by some citizen of Jericho ten thousand years ago?

There *is* a safe, sane, rational explanation for ghosts and it is only a matter of time before twentieth-century science constructs the theoretical model and then the hardware to explain and reveal them.

THE TOURIST TRADE

JUDY HAD CLIMBED TO HER PLACE AT THE breakfast table that morning and announced the presence of a ghost in her room the previous night, a good-looking man ghost who had courteously asked if she were having a nice time.

And Judy's mother, being a sensible, sane American citizen, said nonsense child, there is no such thing as a ghost.

"Well, then," Judy demanded, "who was the man in my bedroom last night, huh?"

Mother looked up from the toast, startled.

"A man, baby?"

"Yes mama. A good-looking man, gooder-looking even than daddy, and he had on a brown uniform like, only it wasn't a soldier's uniform of course but just a uniform."

"A man—with a uniform?"

"Yes mama. A nice man, you know."

"No," Mama contradicted, "I don't know. Are you *sure* you saw a man in your room last night?"

"Sure mama. He was a ghost, a man ghost."

"*Oh*, Judy! Those ghosts again. . . . I've asked you time and again to stop that! There is no such thing as a ghost."

"Well, maybe not mama, but this man come riding in right through my wall on a motor scooter sort of, and he stood up and made a speech like that man said at the museum and he asked me if I was having a nice time."

"All that? Judy!"

"Yes mama. And I told him yes and he said, that's nice, and he set down again and rode the scooter right across my room and went right through my other wall."

"Judy, stop it! You were dreaming."

"Yes mama. The motor scooter didn't make any noise though and he had a uniform on."

"All right, baby. Forget it, darling."

* * *

Judy didn't forget it; she filed the matter away in whatever storage cabinet children have for accumulating knowledge and experiences temporarily unclassified. She filed the matter away, somewhat, until that evening and a new bedtime. Scarcely fifteen minutes after climbing the stairs to bed, she was back down again.

Daddy was hunched in a chair reading a mystery book, fighting off the interfering noise of the radio. Mama was listening to the radio and haphazardly working on a jigsaw puzzle. Judy paused in the doorway of the living room, her pajamas still unmussed, a robe trailing in one hand.

"*Now* what do you want, baby? You should have been asleep ten minutes ago. . . ."

"That man ghost is back again."

"Oh, now Judy! Don't start that again."

"Well, mama, he is, and on top of that he's got some people with him this time, and they're all riding in—"

"Judy!"

"Yes mama?"

"*Up to bed.*"

"Yes mama." The girl turned and slowly climbed the steps. The last of her trailing footsteps sounded on the stairs and presently the bedroom door slammed in its characteristic manner. Mother sighed and looked across the room for help.

"Donald, you've got to *do* something. That child has ghosts on her mind; all I hear is ghosts, ghosts, ghosts. I'm worried about it. Do you think she's been listening to the radio too much?"

Donald wearily raised his eyes from the book. "All kids go through that, forget about it. She's just imaginative, that's all."

"But *such* an imagination—it isn't healthy."

"Oh, bosh. Keep it up and she'll grow up to be an actress, or a writer of something. Listen—" He paused as the opening sound of Judy's bedroom door came to them. The approaching footsteps padded slowly down the stairs.

Judy paused timidly in the doorway, glancing from one parent to the other.

"It's getting late, Judy," daddy spoke up. "Those ghosts again?"

"Yes daddy."

"Won't let you sleep, I suppose?"

"No daddy."

"How many of them, do you think?"

Judy beamed. "Four of them, no five I guess, counting the woman stuck in the wall only she's kinda fuzzy and you can't see her very good. And the man in the uniform."

"Oh, a uniform, eh? And what's *he* doing?"

"He's showing my room to the rest of them and he drives the scooter everybody rides in and he's telling them about my furniture and my dolls and things. Daddy, he don't like it very much."

"Now, really!" Louise broke in.

"Wait a minute, Louise, I'll handle this." He turned his attention to his daughter. "He didn't like your furniture, eh Judy? How do you know that?"

"I could tell by the way he talked, daddy. He said it was Millerya or something and he waved his hand and looked down his nose like you do when you don't like something. Like it wasn't much good, you know. . . ."

"Sure, I know. Millerya, huh? Well, that's too bad. *We* like it, and if he doesn't, he can just jump it, isn't that what you say? What are they going to do next?"

"He wanted to know if there was anybody living in the house beside me."

"Oh, he did eh? Well, you should have told him we were down here."

"I did daddy. And the man in the uniform said for me to come down and tell you they were here."

"I see." He nodded wisely and prepared to wrap it up. "Well, I hate to disappoint your ghost, Judy, but neither your mother or myself feels like climbing the stairs to meet him right now. Will you tell him that for me?"

"Sure thing daddy."

"All right. Good night, Judy."

Judy climbed the stairs at a brisk trot and the bedroom door slammed in its usual fashion. It was opened again and Judy trotted back down just as briskly. She put her head into the living room.

"Daddy?"

"Uh . . . what?" He came up from the depths of the book.

"The ghost says you had better come up there or else."

"Indeed! Or else what?"

"Or else he'll report you."

Donald slammed the book to the floor. Judy jumped in alarm.

"Well daddy, he did, he did!" the girl cried.

"Judy—you get right back up those stairs and tell that ghost I'm *not* coming up to meet him. Not until he plays *Yankee Doodle* on a saxophone. Get that?"

"Yes daddy."

"All right then, get moving. And good night!"

"Good night daddy." The young feet retracing the path up the stairs and the young hands giving the bedroom door a thumping slam. After that the silence from the second floor was a welcome thing.

"There," Donald said in triumph. "I told you I'd handle her. Tact. That's all it takes, tact." He dropped into the overstuffed chair and sought his place in the mystery novel.

From Judy's bedroom came the loud, blaring sound of a saxophone tearing into *Yankee Doodle*.

Donald jumped from the chair and hurled the book across the room, narrowly missing a vase. Removing his belt from his trousers in one angry jerk, he sped for the stairs and bounded upward, two steps at a time. His wife shut her eyes and tried to shut her ears after the bedroom door opened and slammed shut again. The blaring of the saxophone ceased. Nervously, she twiddled a piece of the jigsaw puzzle in her fingers and waited for the blows to fall.

Instead, Donald came down the steps and paused in the doorway.

"Louise—"

"Yes, Donald?"

"The ghost wants you to come up there too."

"Donald!"

"But he insists. He said he wanted to exhibit the whole blamed family, and for you to get up there toot-sweet or he'd report us all. Better come along, Louise."

And he turned to mount the staircase.

"Ah, at last," the uniformed gentleman exclaimed. He turned to address the people waiting behind him, all seated in a low motor conveyance.

"This is a complete family unit of the twentieth century," he announced with evident satisfaction. "They spring from a race of aborigines inhabiting the North American continent from about the fifteenth century through the thirty-third. At the stage of their development you see here, they lived together as a closely-knit family unit in dwelling places they called *houses,* which is a type of building containing many small cells similar to this one. Usually each member of the unit sleeps in a separate cell but they live together in the remainder of those making up the *house*.

"Notice the male. At this early stage of history he has already assumed the place of head of his family unit and is fond of exhibiting various mental and physical characteristics to identify himself as the leader, or chief. Look closely at his face and you will see hair, or fuzz growing. This was known as a *beard* and was permitted to grow to assert independence. These early men were extremely stubborn, as you noted a moment ago when it was necessary to use a musical instrument of the twentieth century to summon him from his cell."

"Go away," Donald said to the uniformed man, "you're bothering us."

"Earlier in the rise of their race, as you will soon see when we move along to the next stop, the aborigines had not yet learned the use of tools and were of course unable to erect buildings such as this one. During that distant period they lived in natural caves, squatting over continual fires for protection from the elements, for warmth, and for cooking. During the present period you see here they had found a means of moving the fires indoors for both warmth and cooking, and also developed a few primitive instruments to assist them in eating. Holding raw food in the fingers has almost vanished in the year before you."

"Well, I like that!" Louise exclaimed.

"G'wan, beat it," Donald chimed in. "It's the kid's bedtime. Shove off."

"This race," the smartly uniformed man continued, "were called Indians, or Americans, the two terms being interchangeable. Sections, or tribes, existed among them and each tribe adopted the name of some patron saint, protective god or robber baron to whom they paid monetary and honorary tribute. Their tribes sometimes bore colorful names like Ohio, Dogpatch, Jones, Republican, and so forth."

"You're a radical," Donald exclaimed. "Now get out of here or I'll put the dog on you!"

"Not too much is known of their social cultures because the various tribes were always warring upon each other, making historical surveys hazardous and the gathering of information extremely difficult. We will make one more stop in this era to observe a gathering of the wise men of the tribes, and there you will see laws and customs being enacted, taxes collected, and so forth. Afterwards, we shall move a bit further along for a quick glimpse of this family's forefathers, and perhaps if we are fortunate we shall see them hunting in the forests with primitive weapons. During that stage of the tour I must remind you to keep your protective shields closed at all times, for occasionally stray bolts from their weapons may drop among us." He paused, and turned to move a small lever.

The conveyance began to move across the room, drawing the misty lady from the confines of the wall to give her a solid, human appearance. The uniformed man cast a glance over his shoulder.

"And so we say good-by to the colorful, romantic twentieth century with its many tribes, its primitive peoples and its quaint customs." He turned to stare at Donald, directing a low-voiced order at the dumbfounded man. "And see that you get here on time after this, chum. No more of that silly saxophone business."

The conveyance wheeled across the room and vanished into the opposite wall, the lady in the rear seat turning for a last amused look at the quaint mill-era furniture. Her face faded and the visitors were gone.

"Donald—" his wife quavered.

"They can't do that to me," Donald roared. "I'm a taxpayer! I'll see my precinct committeeman about this!"

"Wasn't he a nice man, daddy?"

Daddy correctly reasoned that the nice, uniformed man and his strange conveyance of ghostly passengers would be back on the following night. He readied himself accordingly.

A few minutes before Judy's usual bedtime the nose of the vehicle appeared from one wall of the bedroom and the uniformed guide could be seen rising from his seat, preparatory to spouting his lecture on the twentieth-century family unit. He solidified and glanced about the room, noting the absence of Donald's wife and child.

"Come, come, now," he said with displeasure. "Bring in the remainder of your family. We have a nice crowd today."

"I've got a surprise for you," Donald replied softly.

"Indeed?" said the guide. "What?"

"This!" Donald cried, and brought from behind him a double-barreled shotgun. He raised the weapon and fired both barrels at the crowded car. Plaster fountained from the opposite wall and the bedroom window crashed down in shards.

The guide shook his head. "For shame! Please call the family—" he reached behind him to pick up a saxophone— "or must I perform another tune?

"This," he said to the watching tourists, "is a male of the twentieth century. You have just witnessed a primitive fireworks display used by these people to welcome visitors to their land or to celebrate special holidays dedicated to their gods. It would be a generous gesture on our part to show this man we appreciate the display he has prepared for us. Early peoples, you know, thrive on flattery and attention." He broke into a polite applause and the tourists seated behind him took it up. Someone pitched a few coins.

Donald hurled the gun to the floor and stamped on it.

"The twentieth-century man is now beginning his dance of welcome, a tribal ritual which has come down to him from the campfires of his ancestors who roamed the forests still hundreds of years away. I hold in my hand a musical instrument of this age called a saxophone, and presently I will blow a little tune which will summon his mate and child from the nether regions of the building in which they dwell. . . ."

Donald kept trying. On the following night he had laboriously strung a length of hose from the second-floor bathroom to the bedroom, and as the visitors emerged from the wall—a rather thin crowd this particular trip—he attempted to douse them with a strong stream of water. The water squirted through the visitors and splashed down the cracked wall on the opposite side of the room.

"This," said the guide, "is a twentieth-century male. He is welcoming us to his dwelling place with a water ritual designed to wash away the evil spirits which he fears may hamper our coming. When he has thoroughly cleansed the walls of his dwelling and made the unit safe for us, he will begin his dance of welcome and we will be expected to show our appreciation by applause or small gifts and coins. Afterward, by making notes on this instrument in my hand, the remainder of his family will approach. Now, note the quaint furniture of the—"

In an aside as he was leaving, the guide confided to Donald, "Keep it up, chum. You put on the best show on my entire run. We're getting good word-of-mouth advertising."

Donald kept it up. He tried stink bombs, which succeeded only in forcing him and his family out of the house; he brought in a radio, a phonograph, several automobile horns and a borrowed siren in an effort to drive away the tourists from the future by a sheer wall of noise, and succeeded only in blasting his own eardrums; he turned a swarm of bees loose in the room and wound up with numerous stings; he was forcefully prevented by his wife from piling the furniture and the bedding in the room's center and setting fire to it as the guide and his conveyance appeared through the wall.

"This is a man of the twentieth century. He is preparing to welcome us by setting fire to those numerous small red objects you see lying about the floor of the dwelling unit. Presently the red objects will explode with a tremendous repercussion, driving away evil spirits lurking here—he believes—and making our visit a safe one. Now, please note—"

A red-eyed, haggard man stood on a street corner, leaning dazedly against the lamp post. His wife had left him and returned to her mother, declaring that she and their child would return to that horrible house when—and only when—he had rid Judy's room of those horrible visitations once and for all. He hadn't reported for work for over a week and his job was in danger; he hadn't slept for the same length of time and his health was in similar jeopardy. His friends avoided him, believing he had fallen into the clutches of the demon rum. All in all, he was a sad specimen of twentieth-century man. And he was on the mental verge of ending it all when the bus went by.

Someone babbling in a loud voice caught his attention and he glanced up, cringing instinctively at the sight of a rubberneck bus wheeling along the street. Sick at heart, he turned his back to discover passers-by gazing curiously back at the bus.

Donald opened his eyes wide.

The low-bodied motor conveyance began its nightly appearance through the wall, and Donald saw the guide rising from his seat to address the tourists behind him. Donald folded his arms and waited. The entire vehicle came into view, well-crowded, and stopped.

The uniformed guide looked at him inquiringly.

"Pretty quiet around here, chum. Can't you whip up something?"

"I certainly can, mister," Donald told him. "Just you wait right here." He crossed to the bedroom door and flung it open, jumping back to avoid the mob. "Here they are folks," he shouted, *"as* advertised." Holding out his hat, he admitted the crowd into the room, watching carefully to see that each dropped a coin into the receptacle.

"Real, genuine ghosts, folks, the only haunted house in Libertyville! Each night and every night on the hour this ghostly crew rides out of that wall yonder and parades across the room. Step right up to them folks, try to touch them, try to feel them. You can't! Come right in and meet my ghosts."

The small bedroom was suddenly filled with awed, milling people crowding forward to gaze at the ghostly conveyance. Curious hands reached out to touch the future tourists, only to grasp the empty air. Flash guns popped as newspaper photographers snapped what they hoped would be pictures of the visitation. A representative of the American Ethereal Society pinched his glasses to his nose and held a lighted match to the ghostly guide's natty uniform, testing to see if flaming gauze netting would reveal a trickery. The guide stared at the flashbulbs, slightly taken aback.

"Come now," he said, "this will be reported."

"He talks, he walks, he plays a saxophone!" Donald shouted above the din. "A real, genuine ghost, folks, step right up and take a look at the real article!"

"Where in hell did they come from?" a reporter wanted to know, brazenly pushing two fingers into and through the disapproving face of the guide. "I'm damned if they scare me!"

"He's a legend connected with the house," Donald explained glibly. "According to the story, this fellow in the uniform was an eccentric inventor who used to live here but he finally killed himself. The story says he was a 4-F but he wore that uniform to ease his conscience; he always claimed to be inventing war machines for the government. See all those people behind him?"

Necks craned to look at the tourists.

"They were *murdered!*" Donald whispered hoarsely. "According to the legend, this crazy inventor murdered them all and sealed their bodies up in the wall. And now, every night, he lines up all the ghosts on this crazy machine he imagines he invented and rides them through the walls. . . ."

A fresh onslaught of people in the doorway drew his attention. Snatching up the hatful of jingling coins, Donald fought his way to the door.

"Step right in, folks, the ghosts are here! Come right in and meet genuine ghosts in the only haunted house in town! Each night and every night—"

Donald's wife and child returned home the following weekend. Judy was installed in a new bedroom, and in due time developed an intense interest in Hopalong Cassidy.

If you are a male would you like to be married to a crocodile? Or perhaps a djinni?

If you are married, and a male, how do you know that your spouse really is a human female? Or would you rather not find out?

MY BROTHER'S WIFE

THERE ARE THREE OF US—THREE BROTHERS.
Harley is the oldest of the trio and in many ways the weakest. The family had been in the habit of telling each other Harley would go far someday. Harley went as far as a downstate mental asylum. He's been in there for several months and I can't get in to see him, not with the family balking me, not with my record.

Louise put him there.

Jimmy is the youngest, he's a born hell-raiser but strictly on the legit side. The kind of a guy you don't have to dare to do something—he will plunge in and tackle it just for the hell of the thing. But it has to be on the level. He uses *me* as the shining example of what not to be. Jimmy was in the air force during the war and spent most of his time overseas flying the Hump, messing around in some of those nameless pockets in Burma. He likes to brag about the time he flew Stilwell.

Jimmy is married to Louise. I don't see her, either.

In age, I'm between those two brothers but there is no other resemblance, and as any member of the family will tell you in nice language, I'm not worth a tinker's dam. The old black sheep label was pinned on me early—a stretch in the reform school when I was seventeen because I had figured out a way to make, and use, a black powder bomb after watching a Paul Muni gangster picture. And a lush but rugged pre-war life out on Chicago's southwest side while toting a gun for a ward heeler, at the magnificent sum of a hundred bucks a week.

That was all washed up when they drafted me; the only thing that changed was the clothes and the pay. I went right on toting a gun for thirty bucks a month and grub until Congress got big hearted and raised the pay. And I got smart and bought me a softer job driving a car for the brass.

I'm back on my own now, working for nobody but myself and still carrying a gun for sentimental reasons. I've been waiting a long time to get my sights on Jimmy's wife.

People tell me she's a knock-out, something a movie scout should stumble over. I wouldn't know—I've never laid eyes on her although she and the kid brother have lived in Chicago for over a year. He runs his own bookstore down near the Loop, something he bought with the money he saved up during the war plus his discharge dough. When I first found out what he wanted, I made it a little easier for him to buy out the former owner at a reasonable price. I keep a boy down there working for him to see nothing goes wrong—some dope might get the bright idea that a bookstore, like a dry cleaning joint, could be in the market for protection.

I am *not* welcome in his house unless she is away from home. So I always telephone in advance.

I drop around for an evening of bull and beer every once in a while to pick up the news on Harley and the folks, and to study Jimmy. We get along fine and he'd be a helluva swell guy to chin with if only he'd shut up that bragging about what he did in the war. I keep wondering what he's thinking about and never find out. I always ask him how the store is coming along and is he making any money, and he usually tells me it's rolling in—which I already know. But he never says a word about how he's getting along with her and he never asks about my business. We leave it at that, but I keep wondering.

I usually slip him some dough and he passes it along to the family with a donation of his own, because we both know Mom would refuse it if she guessed it was coming from me. Once in a while he has a fresh word on Harley but it is always bad—the guy will never snap out of it. And that's the point of the matter.

Louise is responsible for Harley being in the hatch, and I keep wondering if Jimmy knows that.

I used to ask about her, back at the beginning. Used to wonder out loud when I'd get to meet my nifty new sister-in-law, used to pass out hints I was entitled to a kiss. He became embarrassed every time I brought up the subject. He parried my questions with unsatisfactory answers and offered all kinds of feeble excuses for her continued absence. The hints brought me nothing but pained silences.

After a while I began to get the idea and one night I asked him about it.

"I never have seen her, kid. What's the inside—that black sheep stuff again?"

He avoided my eyes and wasted several seconds reading the small print on the beer label. Somewhere in the house a gnawing rodent sounded loud in the silence.

"Come on," I coaxed him, "I'm not going to get mad."

He jerked back his shoulders and stared at me. I had the answer before he opened his mouth.

"I'm awfully sorry, Bud. I guess I opened my mouth once too often, or maybe Mom tipped her off, I don't know. I guess she's afraid of you, Bud. It's a crazy idea and I've told her a hundred times you're my own brother and wouldn't hurt a fly, but—well, you know women."

Yeah, I knew women, knew lots of them, but she was the first one I'd found who was afraid to shake hands with me. It didn't sound right, didn't tie in with her background; she'd hung around plenty of tough characters in the Burma country.

"She's seen too many bad movies," he went on, "or read too many books I guess—even over there. She thinks you're a cross between a bloody newspaper gangster and a storm trooper." He ran his hand through his hair and there was something else on his mind, something he didn't tell me. He was embarrassed. "I can't help it, Bud, and I apologize for it, but hell, that's the way it is."

That was the way it was.

By "even over there" he meant her homeplace, somewhere in Burma or India or wherever the hell he picked her up. He said once it was a mudtown called Walawbum but I couldn't find it on a map. He found her there and I suppose you can find anything and everything in that country if you stay long enough; she was, he told me later, a half caste of some sort, Russian and Chinese maybe, who had drifted around here and there with the coming of the Japanese war to the mainland.

If she was a half caste, I pointed out, how come the name Louise? He laughed and told me I couldn't pronounce her real name if I tried, so everybody called her Louise. Jimmy was positive on one point; she was as attractive as they come. The family took her in when he brought her home, which was equal to an underwriter's bond unless she mesmerized them.

"Well hell, kid," I said, "it's tough, not so much as getting to see her. Hey—got a picture around anywhere?"

He gave me a lopsided grin, half an apology and half a defense. "No, Bud. I'm sorry, but I can't even offer you that much. She won't stand still for it. She's the best wife in this whole cockeyed world today—she'll do anything for me, except that. She won't let me take her picture."

"What?"

"Nope, on the level. You see, that was one of the things she brought up when I married her." He broke off to stare at me, wondering just how much he could say. "To make it plain, Bud, before I could marry her I had to promise no pix. That was her one and only condition of marriage. I can't go back on my promise."

He wouldn't. I knew him too well for that.

"Religion or something?" I asked him.

He nodded absently. "I suppose so. She's from the backwoods over there, you know. People aren't so particular about what goes on around them but you'd better not step on their taboos. I married *her*, not her superstitions or whatever. She's got a lot of funny little tricks you'll never find out here in the civilized world, and I like every one of them."

I said I guessed I understood.

"She told me her ancestors would never forgive her if she permitted a photograph to be taken. And Bud, I don't want to get her in a jam with her ancestors." He was grinning at me in high humor but it faded. "I'm head over heels in love with her—and I don't want that to be jammed, either."

So I dropped the subject and kept hoping I'd meet her accidentally sometime, but I never did.

Harley had been different—Harley had come and gone as he pleased, when he pleased, saw her quite a lot. He went out with them, stayed in evenings with them, everybody got along fine. Until that night Jimmy called me from home to say the cops had carted Harley away to the hatch.

I suppose I could have stolen a picture of her, could have put a camera tail on her, or I could have tailed her myself and stopped her in the street if I wanted to go that far—but I didn't. Jimmy would raise hell and cut me off. And I didn't want that; his continued friendship and now my only contact with the family meant more to me than just satisfying my curiosity about his wife's looks. I didn't fully accept his explanation of the woman's refusal to meet me, but I said to hell with the whole thing and kept my nose to the grindstone.

Meanwhile I had developed a lead in the asylum.

I wasn't allowed inside. The family laid down the law there and my Cook County record backed them up, so I did the next best thing and picked up a man who was already on the inside. State employees are notoriously underpaid and this one was a greedy bugger who was more than willing to supplement his income, once I convinced him I wanted nothing more than reports on Harley. I began to get them. How he was getting along, his lack of real progress toward recovery, his flights of fancy, his treatment at the hands of the employees, and so forth.

His flights of fancy interested me. They always included Louise. He was crazy about Louise. Crazy.

He talked about her all the time and the words and sentences which were passed along to me didn't make sense. They made just as little sense to his doctors and his progress chart never improved. I put that down as natural in his condition until some of the words, coming in almost daily repetition, bored into me as being queerly unnatural. The more I mulled them over the more curious I grew as to what prompted them. I realized my lead wasn't enough.

The guy had a daily contact with Harley, he could pick up words like a phonograph record and play them back to me just as straight, he could look after him and steer him clear of some of the knocks, but he wasn't sufficiently informed to discuss Harley's case with me. I needed a doctor in the institution and most doctors followed their stupid code of ethics. Which meant I couldn't simply pick up the telephone and ask.

I looked over the hospital staff and began working on a new lead. He lived in Chicago, he wouldn't exchange his ethics for my money until he had great need of it. That might take several weeks, but I started in. A thief stole his car. Someone broke into his house one night and ruined his medical library. He was held up twice in one month. It went along like that and I bided my time.

But while I waited for him to soften I started backtracking.

Jimmy and Louise had lived for some months in San Diego after his discharge, and had then moved on to Phoenix. They spent a couple of years in Phoenix, finally coming to Chicago when the bookstore deal opened up and he decided it was his life. San Diego wouldn't be so difficult —I knew contacts there—but Phoenix was something else again.

In the end I hired a private eye to investigate the Phoenix story, and telephoned a friend in San Diego to look into things there. Some weeks went by and the Phoenix reply arrived first—the detective did a good job. Jimmy and his wife had lived there long enough to make an impression on the neighbors.

Jimmy was the same old Jimmy, in Phoenix. But Louise was somebody else. I kept Harley in mind and studied it.

Jimmy, according to the detective's innocent report, had been living with a different woman while in Arizona, but one who passed as his wife of course. Her name was Louise —the neighbors said she was a perfect darling. The Louise in Phoenix was painted so clearly in the report that I was able to picture her as I read it. Five-foot-one, about a hundred pounds, perhaps twenty-three years old, deep auburn hair worn in bangs, ice-blue eyes, freckled face, upturned nose, small mouth, slim neck, moderate bust, no appreciable hips, tiny feet, lively and vivacious. A carefree and childish manner, a casual dresser—usually slacks and shirt —and occasionally a dramatic burst of temper.

But that wasn't the Louise living in Chicago.

Several days afterward the man in San Diego called. It had been tougher there, their stay had been a shorter one, the neighbors not so observant, and many years had passed. The meager description my contact furnished said Jimmy was still Jimmy in San Diego, but Louise . . .

Louise was a raven-haired beauty with a throaty voice and a figure to make you turn and stare. The apartment house manager remembered her because she had looked like Joan Bennett in the movies; there was such a striking resemblance that he had once asked for an autograph and had been rudely turned down. He remembered her beautiful black hair.

But that wasn't the Louise in Chicago, either.

Jimmy says she's a feast for the eyes—what he has always dreamed of. The tall, willowy girl you find in advertising models, a wealth of hair the color of ripe wheat on a bright summer day, hair that draped about her shoulders. She is almost as tall as Jimmy and he is five-foot-ten, she has the ice-blue eyes of the girl in Phoenix but the straight nose and gentle, curving lips of someone else. Skin as fine and clear as a child's, without a mar or blemish—no freckles. Rather flat-chested, as may be expected of a woman with her build, and a small hip line. That was Louise in Chicago.

Jimmy had changed wives three times and they were all the same girl—he pretended—that he had brought home from the Orient. Picture a half caste as a redhead with freckles, or a tall slim blonde. He had married her in Burma—he pretended—and she would stand for no nonsense about photographs. But he spent a lot of time thinking over something. My other brother, Harley, would be spending the rest of his life in an asylum because Louise had a lot of funny little tricks you'd never find out here in the civilized world.

It was time to pay another visit to his house. And as usual I phoned first that I was coming over, and as usual she was nowhere to be seen when I arrived. Jimmy and I settled in the kitchen with the beer. And somewhere a mouse or a rat was still raising hell in the woodwork.

"Say, kid, your wedding anniversary is coming up pretty soon, ain't it? What do you and the wife want?"

"Is it?" He frowned, put down the can of beer and counted his fingers. "By gosh, you're right. It slipped my mind. Aw—we don't need anything."

"That's not the point, you're going to get something just the same. What'll it be?" I laughed. "A jar of freckle cream for Louise?"

"She doesn't have freckles. You—" and he stopped in embarrassment, realizing that I did not know her face.

"The hell she doesn't! You said she did."

"I did? You're all wet, Bud. Her skin's like milk."

"Well, maybe I am, but I'd swear you said freckles in one of those old letters—from Phoenix I think, some time back."

He shook his head and traced a design on the table top, a long snaky line. "Guess I was mixed up, or you read it wrong. No freckles." He tried to keep the concern off his face.

"Skip it," I suggested. "Name something nice, then."

He was morose the rest of the evening and I got out of there early.

*   *   *

Harley was far gone—he had been put away for nearly a year with positively no sign of improvement—when my doctor finally got around to my point of view. It had taken him a long time to throw off the inner feeling that he was betraying himself and his profession, that he was accepting rotten money, but he finally reached the desperate stage when he could sit down and talk to me without too many mental reservations.

"What about Harley?" I asked him.

"Incurable. You should know that."

"Sure I know it. That's not why I'm here. I'm here to find out why Harley went that way, what caused it? You've listened to him."

"Your brother, Mr. Wyatt, is suffering from rather common causes which affect a good many people in today's world, and that is the root of it. The world and its emotions are moving too fast, far too fast for some of us, and he was one of those who could not keep his footing. He stumbled. It happens about us every day, I regret to say. Modern life is too involved, too complex and unyielding in its demands, for some men to handle with ease. They simply fail under the load—it is a retreat from a life they cannot or do not wish to cope with."

"Keep the lectures for the old folks, Doc. I'm asking about Harley."

"Harley is—" he broke off and frowned. "Precisely what are you seeking, Mr. Wyatt?"

"Things. Have you met my sister-in-law, Louise Wyatt?"

"No, I'm afraid I haven't. I've heard of her, of course."

I shot him a glance. "I'll say you've heard of her. Harley raves about her all the time. What about that?"

He was instantly ill at ease and sought to avoid an answer. Some of those mental reservations again.

"Well? What about it?"

"Eh . . . I believe he does mention the woman."

"You bet he does—have you listened to him?"

"Naturally I attempt to understand my—"

I broke in. "Have you listened to him?"

"Yes. Yes I have."

"Sounds screwy, doesn't it?"

"Which is why he is under our care, Mr. Wyatt."

"Yeah," I said. "Anybody who carries on like that is asking to be locked up. Where does he get those ideas—

about a woman who changes her shape to look like somebody else?"

The doctor stared at me and wondered just how much he could say. I guessed his mind, made an impatient gesture.

He said slowly, "Frankly, Mr. Wyatt, your brother's troubles seem to arise from an . . . ah, fixation upon the person of your sister-in-law. I have reason to believe his mental unbalance came about when he possibly . . . ah, declared his love for her and she spurned him, of course. He perhaps accompanied his declaration of affections with some desperate plan for the two of them to run away someplace. Naturally, it never occurred to him that she would refuse, but when she did he was so overwrought he lost possession of his faculties."

"Boiling that down, you mean he blew his top when she laughed at him."

"That is correct."

"And then what?"

"In a given situation such as this we may expect one of two subsequent possibilities. The patient either continues to love the object of his affection by mentally refusing her declination, or he approaches a natural opposite and dislikes her violently. The latter, I may add, happens rather often in everyday life but the spurned lover seldom comes to our attention because he is able to assimilate the load, either by recourse to liquor, physical exertion or simply forgetting the woman.

"Only occasionally are they brought to us; more often they find themselves in jail for assault upon the body of the woman, or their more successful rival."

"Harley was really nuts about Louise?"

"Yes, I believe so."

"And now, I suppose, he hates her guts?"

"Yes. In his mind's desire to seek revenge upon her he is mentally casting her into all sorts of unflattering moulds and evil guises, wishing upon her every imaginable kind of ugly form—a snake perhaps, or a lizard, a rat, or some other predatory animal or reptile."

I let that soak in and again wondered what was on Jimmy's mind. In some of our recent kitchen conversations he had been a mile away from me.

"I take it that you don't pay much attention to his ravings—about Louise being a different woman?"

"Of course not. We—" The doctor broke off to stare at me. "You have put that rather oddly, Mr. Wyatt."

I took the report from the Phoenix detective out of my pocket and handed it over to him.

"Read this, Doc. If I told you what I meant by that crack, you'd try to lock me up too."

He skimmed through it, smiling.

"This seems to concern your brother James, and his wife."

"Yeah. It concerns her, mostly. There's an accurate description in there of the woman when she lived in Phoenix. Too bad you haven't met her here, in Chicago."

"Why do you say that?"

"Because she looks like this now—" and I gave him a full picture description of Louise as she appeared now. By this time he had read the Phoenix descriptions.

"A different woman, obviously," he said, still smiling.

Finally I told him what she was like in San Diego. He shook his head.

"I dislike to insert myself into family affairs, Mr. Wyatt, but apparently your brother has been living with three separate women, each of whom posed as his wife and used the same name. It's done, of course."

"Of course. But I see you don't connect this up with Harley's ravings?"

He glanced at me rather sharply. "Of course not!"

"No," I echoed with open sarcasm, "of course not. Did you ever hear of a case of a woman changing her shape—form?"

He was now smiling broadly.

"I believe I see your objective quite clearly, sir. Yes, I've heard of such things—in mythology. Let me see . . . there are witch-women who may change their shape at will; there are were-wolves and were-tigers, that is, half human and half tiger who may assume the guise of a beguiling woman; oh, there are any number of fantastic creatures in mythology who use a human form to gain some immediate goal or mislead some poor man. I should point out, however, that that is mythology."

"Harley's pretty far gone on that one idea," I said. "Maybe he's been reading the fantasy books."

The doctor thought I was serious. "It is possible, yes. A great deal of mythology is taught children, fairy tales and that sort of thing. Some modern fiction employs it as a base. *Dracula* is a case in point. And many magazines to-day cater to the adult who hasn't fully left the fairy tale behind him. Something of that sort may have given your brother the idea of casting the woman into different moulds."

"How about the chance," I asked softly, "of Harley actually having seen something? Something different?"

The doctor pin-pointed me. "Oh, not a chance! Superstitions belong to the old world, to Europe and Africa." He was watching me closely. I could guess his thoughts.

"And India maybe," I agreed, "or Burma."

"India is teeming with superstition."

I got up—this guy was a blank wall. "Sorry to take up so much of your time, Doc. I guess that's that. The stuff got on my mind and I had to talk to somebody about it. I had to see if there was anything behind Harley's raving."

"Just be careful, Mr. Wyatt, that it doesn't weigh too heavily on your mind. Our population out there is always increasing." He pointed to the detective's report. "By the way, did by chance your brother Harley read this document?"

"Thinking maybe *that* sent him off? No, I picked this up a couple of months ago, didn't get started on it until he was locked up and started talking about a different woman. Ties in, don't it Doc?

"I don't leave nothing to chance, I can't afford to. And listen, as a matter of curiosity, supposing these witch-women could change their shape from one woman to another, supposing *one* of them was a brunette in San Diego and a little redheaded squirt in Phoenix and still something else in Chicago? Supposing all these women were the same woman, just changing around to please her husband—you know, give him a taste of everything? How could you tell which woman was the real one?"

"What?"

"Which one of those three is the real McCoy, with the others just window dummies?"

That one sent him off into a spasm of laughter.

When he quieted again, he said, "It isn't a question of discovering the true woman, Mr. Wyatt. I'm afraid you weren't listening closely. The problem there, if such a problem existed, would be to discover the true *form* from which the woman sprang. She would not be a woman at base."

"Oh? No?"

"No. At base she would be an animal, reptile or bird. She would be a woman when the object of her intentions, a man, first saw her. Afterwards, depending upon whether or not the man discovered part or all of her secret, she might assume the forms of various other women to please him. In the twinkling of an eye she could become the image of almost any woman on earth that he desired."

"All dames in the body of one, eh?"

"All women in the body of something," he corrected me. "You would never discover which woman-shape was the basic one because *none* were. The pretty face of the fairy tale is but a snarling beast beneath—a tiger, a crocodile."

Or, I thought to myself after I left the doctor, a monkey, or a rattlesnake, or a cockroach, or an ant eater, or a wolf, or the rat I always heard gnawing in the walls. Jimmy's wife had a lot of funny little tricks you'd never find in the outside world. Jimmy said so.

He had also told me he was head over heels in love with her, meaning all three of her I guess.

I could put a man in the house with a camera, using infra-red film and flash bulbs for night work. Neither of them would see the flash and take alarm but she might hear the noise of the shutter and I wouldn't get my picture. I'd not only lose the picture, I'd lose Jimmy—he'd know.

In the end I decided to risk it myself.

A midnight fire next door to the downtown bookstore cleared the way; someone telephoned and the lights went on in their bedroom. Scarcely five minutes later Jimmy came running out of the house half dressed, half awake. He whipped the car out of the garage, backed to the street, and with a farewell toot on the horn vanished with a roar of exhaust.

I waited behind the garage a full half hour before letting myself in the kitchen door, to pad across the room in stocking feet. The lights in the bedroom had long ago been turned off and the house was quiet. I hoped I had given her time to go back to sleep, to relax her vigilance now that he was gone. And I found myself wondering why she had always avoided me.

Harley had been welcome at the house and Jimmy had taken her to visit the family often enough. But she had refused to see me, to let me see her. Jimmy's vague excuses about my past, my present, weren't entirely acceptable. She was afraid of me for some other reason, for some strong reason. She might fear me because I wasn't weak, like Harley; or moonstruck, like her husband; or fawning, like the family. She might fear me because I could see through the body she was wearing.

I stopped just outside the bedroom door and listened. No sound. Carefully, avoiding the noise of scuffling, I put my shoes back on and then eased the snout of my gun around the doorframe, pointing at where I judged the bed to be. There was no movement from within.

I waited a few seconds and followed the gun with my eyes.

They had become used to the semi-darkness of the house, and I saw the room distinctly in the little light seeping in from the street. The bed was over by the windows and it had not been slept in. Startled, I looked around the room for Louise and saw no sign of her.

Without thinking, I stepped in the bedroom and flicked the wall switch.

There was a swift, frightened movement from the far side of the room and something ran across the floor, seeking the safety of darkness under the bed. I jumped for it, ran between it and the bed, and as it sought to dodge around me, stepped on it.

It never occured to me to use the gun still in my hand. My first instinct had been to step on it, to smash out its life, and I had done so. I scraped the sole of my shoe clean on a rug and snapped off the bedroom light.

I went back to the kitchen. In the darkness I pulled a chair around facing the door and sat down with the gun in my hand, waiting for Jimmy to come home.

Their bed had not been slept in—neither of them used it.

The ideal mystery story (even in science fiction) should contain a seeker-after-truth who works with none but the scantiest of clues and a minimum of hardware, a beautiful woman who is not always what she seems but is perpetually in danger, and a dastardly villain who plots the demise of the seeker and the seizure of the woman. An evil alien bent on enslaving the world is an added attraction.

The job is ended and the mystery solved only when the seeker cleverly uses his few clues to track down the villain in his lair and rescue the beautiful woman in the nick of time. Sometimes the world is also saved.

If you choose to believe all that, I can sell you weed seeds for your garden.

THE JOB IS ENDED

THE MOMENT I SAW MARIE JACKSON I KNEW I was finished. At last, a thirty-year search was over, a suspicious man's theory had become a fact, and a laboratory problem was solved. Marie Jackson brought it to a close.

Strangely enough, it was her husband who had betrayed her to me, and gave me the first hint that the job was nearing its finish.

The secondary discovery was as strange as the first and was the one thing I had not been expecting. Marie Jackson was a woman . . . I had been searching for a man. For thirty years I had been hunting down a man, any man who happened to fit the specifications of a laboratory theory. My instructions from Brigham in Washington had been to search for a man who didn't belong, who, if he *did* fit the specifications, would prove that the theory was an actual fact and that Earth did have a visitor. Instead of a man I turned up Marie Jackson, and I made ready to close the case.

Arthur Jackson wandered into my office one warm June day wearing his troubles on his face.

A second look revealed that he wasn't merely having domestic troubles, but was drowning his miseries. It was in his walk, it hung from his shoulders, and it preyed on his mind constantly. He failed to see my outstretched hand —I don't believe he saw *me* very clearly. He sat down across the desk from me and ran a palm over his moist forehead. Nashville in the summer was insufferably hot, but Jackson was suffering from more than the heat.

He was well dressed, though his suit was wrinkled, and he crushed a hat in his hand. He wasn't soft by any measure, he had no paunch, his fingers were long and sure, and the nails reasonably clean. His eyes were intelligent enough behind the blanket of worry, and his hairline was beginning to recede. Jackson wore a small *ACT* pin in his lapel, which was what tipped me off that he was an Oak Ridge man. The American Chemical Trust runs things out there for the government.

Finally he looked me straight in the eye. "People say you're pretty reliable, Mr. Evans."

I shrugged and waited.

"I read about you in the papers a few Sundays ago," he continued. "That was why I came to you. The papers said you had never lost a case, Mr. Evans. That is, they said you have found every man you've ever hunted."

"Sunday supplement stuff," I told him.

"But it *is* true?" he persisted.

"Reasonably so," I nodded. "Those I couldn't locate later proved to be dead."

"I'm having trouble, Mr. Evans," he said uselessly. "The paper—well, perhaps it *was* melodramatic, but it claimed your deductive powers were uncanny. Pardon me, Mr. Evans—it said you could almost read minds. You would have to be a mind reader to find my wife!"

I smiled at him in modest depreciation. "You know the newspapers, Mr. Jackson." I paused for the right length of time. "How much do you want to tell me?"

He stared up at me again, directly into my eyes. The words rushed out eagerly.

"Everything, I want to tell you everything, Mr. Evans, but you probably won't believe me. *They* didn't."

"Who didn't?"

"My doctor, and a psychiatrist recommended by the doctor." He pulled out a handkerchief to wipe his forehead. "I went to the doctor first because I grew up in the habit of taking everything to my doctor. I could have saved myself the trouble," he added bitterly.

"And the psychiatrist?" I prodded gently.

"Practically the same. A mild neurosis, he told me. Said I would probably be completely happy in a matriarchy, but there was nothing to worry about. He did assure me that I was reasonably sane—I suppose I should be thankful for that."

"And so," I put in, "you turned to me."

"Yes—" he was staring at me intently. "Will you do me a favor, Mr. Evans, a very great favor?"

"If I am able, yes."

"Please—" the words came tumbling out again. "Don't laugh at me. Don't laugh at what I have to tell you. Don't pat my shoulder and tell me I am imagining things, that I need a long rest. If you choose not to believe me, I'll leave. Refuse my case and stop right there. But don't laugh."

"That much is easily granted. Where are you going to begin?"

"With my wife. Everything begins with my wife—and ends there, I'm afraid. She's—" he hesitated, stole a glance at me, and finished, "she's too damned smart!"

He waited for my reaction but I showed none.

"Have you ever had the misfortune to marry a woman far more intelligent than yourself, Mr. Evans?"

I shook my head. "Not married."

He rushed on. "You can imagine what a man desires in a woman. Among other things, the usual physical things, he wants a smart and intelligent wife, a woman possessing mental abilities sufficient to understand him and his world. A woman who can stride along with him, and understand his problems. But still, and this is a paradox I'll admit, a woman necessarily inferior to him—the least bit inferior, sort of a balance of ego. A man wants a woman who needs his advice, who needs to lean on him, who needs his greater reasoning powers. That is the kind of woman every healthy man desires, Mr. Evans. I thought I had found such a woman in Marie."

I stared past him out the window, at the sunlit street and an idea formed in my mind. "How old is your wife?" I asked him, and his answer was my first clue to her, although it went unrecognized as such, right then.

"We don't know, really." He seemed embarrassed. "She is an orphan and we couldn't locate a birth registration—the situation stirred up a bit of a fuss when I started with the Manhattan people as they looked into everything, you know. Marie and I agreed when we married that she was about five years younger than myself." He paused in thought. "That would make her thirty-two now . . . we think. Sometimes I'm not sure. She hasn't grown much older than the day—— Her physical appearance bears that out, Mr. Evans. Thirty-two."

I knew that to be a half-truth for he wasn't sure in his own mind. "And you?" I asked. "You're a success in your field?"

He absently fingered the lapel pin and nodded. Jackson told me about himself, about Manhattan in the days before we got into the war, and afterward: About Oak Ridge now and his position there, the full, fruitful years of his life; about the growing unhappiness and strain between himself and his wife, about his striving to overcome it. He wound up by asserting, "I consider myself an intelligent man, Mr. Evans. You'll grant me that, leaving false modesty aside."

I agreed without quibbling. "Easily granted." He had told me far more than he realized and I could honestly agree with the statement. "But now—back to your wife?"

"Yes, my wife."

He lapsed into what must have been a painful silence for him and his mind skittered back over those years, tracing the early ripening of his love for her. He made it easy for me to follow him although I was careful to give no outward sign of that; I waited patiently for him to speak. I saw him as a young man holding down a modest-paying position, a young man with reasonable security—a future, and a desire—the not unnatural desire to find a wife to share that future. He discovered Marie in a library.

"In the evenings after work," he finally broke the silence, "I studied the technical books and journals I could not yet afford. I wanted to climb as rapidly and as safely as possible and I realized that if I waited until I could afford those books, it might be too late.

"I met her in the library. She was looking at a schematic drawing in an early radio journal, tracing it with her finger. It startled me when I looked closely to see what she was really doing, and at the same time it pleased me. You must realize it was—and is—very unusual to find a woman interested in such things; I stood behind her chair and watched her finger. She went along splendidly for a few moments and then ran into trouble.

"I don't recall now what it was, but it threw her entirely off the track and caused her to lose the thread of thought as well. I could determine that much by the way she reacted. When you lose the thought behind a schematic you may as well start over again." He paused to look at me."

"I understand what you mean. Go on."

He continued. "Well—she pushed the journal away with a whispered exclamation of annoyance and started to get up. And I, like a damned fool, had to butt in; I leaned over her shoulder and pointed to the trouble spot.

" 'No, *this* way,' I remember saying to her impulsively, and then I stopped and could say no more. She threw me one withering glance over her shoulder and I hurriedly left the library, in some confusion I must admit. She disturbed me."

"Was it an act?" I wanted to know.

"Act? You mean, was she pretending? No, I don't think so. She was an utter stranger to me. I avoided the library on the following night because I still felt some embarrassment, but on the third evening an overpowering desire to see her again swept away any misgivings I may have had. The desire amounted almost to a pull, a compulsion. She still disturbed me."

I pricked up my ears and senses. I was beginning to learn things about Jackson's wife.

He said, "I went back to the library . . ."

". . . and there she was," I finished for him. He misinterpreted me, and thought I was asking a question.

"Yes. I found her studying a book I had turned in only a few weeks previously. It was a field closely allied to my own, can you understand that? It had not been easy going for me but there she sat, working through it. I was astonished and I was delighted—and although I carefully avoided her that evening and continued to do so for several nights thereafter, eventually . . . well, Mr. Evans, eventually the attraction to her overcame my reticence. I can't explain it more clearly."

"No need," I assured him. "Easily understandable, and it happens all the time. Mutual interest in your sciences, each of you obviously alone—" I let it hang there.

He nodded. "Yes, yes, I finally summoned up my courage, approached her and introduced myself. She was not angry." He closed his eyes, dreaming. "In time we became fast friends. We met there several times, and elsewhere. In a very short while I began to entertain ideas. Frankly, they surprised me for up until that moment I had been rather shy where women were concerned, but Marie's presence seemed to invite ideas."

I'll just bet—I said to myself.

"I thought," he went on without a pause, "she was—or rather she would be—what any intelligent man might call a perfect wife. She was endowed with everything I could ask in a mate, including the remarkable intelligence I desired in my dream woman. I . . . I may as well make this brief. We were married."

I turned from the window to face the man. He was looking at me, waiting for my reaction thus far.

"Jackson," I said, throwing it at him, "you were hooked."

"Uh . . . hooked?"

"Hooked," I nodded without a smile, "but don't be alarmed, *that* goes on all the time, too. A million women employ a million ways to *hook* a million men. Quite common."

He wasn't alarmed at my words, he merely went off on another dream train. His voice trailed off and drifted back across the years to their marriage.

He married her because he was madly in love with her, with her body, her beauty, her soul and her intelligence quotient. He married her because he would have something few men could boast—an alert, brainy woman who was practically his equal in any field he chose to explore. He married her because she could read a schematic, *but* ran into trouble on certain parts of it. That iota of necessary inferiority was there. He married her because she would be a valuable asset to his own standing and mentality. And somewhere along the line, between the honeymoon and the present day, the glorious bubble burst. I saw it blow up in his face as he relived it in his mind.

"Which brings us to the present," I reminded him, jolting him out of his silence.

"Yes," he echoed bitterly, "the present. Mr. Evans, I love my wife."

You are a liar, I said to him, but *not* aloud. He didn't *love* his wife any more; it was something else now, something akin to love but definitely not affection. However, I said nothing, it wouldn't do for me to call his cards.

"Still married?" I prodded.

He nodded unhappily.

"Exactly why did you come to me?" I demanded of him.

Arthur Jackson stared at me. I had forced the crisis on him and had already read his answer, but still had to wait for his torrent of words.

"Because Marie has surpassed me," he almost cried, "out-stripped me because she is an unimaginable distance ahead." He held up a hand. "No—please, don't mistake me. I'm not mad, not angry, I'm jealous, yes, terribly jealous. But all that aside, Mr. Evans, she won't let me see her."

"Other men?" I wanted to know.

"I don't know; I suppose so. She has moved out of our home and lives at some hotel. These other men—if they exist—I've never seen them, I can only suspect they exist. But that isn't what is bothing me. I can't *see* her!"

I caught something there which was startling.

"What was that?"

"Mr. Evans, in the many years we lived together, Marie sucked my mind of knowledge like a bat sucks blood. Everything I've learned in the past ten years she *knew* the following day! I would spend weeks working through a technological problem and she would know the full answer in one evening at the dinner table. I just couldn't keep anything from her."

"Wait a moment," I cut in impatiently, "let's get back to your first statement. What do you mean, you can't see her?"

"Mr. Evans—" he groped in a mental darkness, stammering. "Mr. Evans, you won't believe me, but—well, Marie blanks out."

I couldn't pretend that didn't shake me, couldn't hide my reaction from him. The shock reflected on my face. He was watching that face for disbelief, but whatever else he found there, it wasn't disbelief. Even though his earlier conversation had prepared me by laying the foundations, this was still a jolt. A jolt curiously marked with wonder, plus the birth of desire.

So Marie Jackson "blanks out." How very interesting. She did not have a birth certificate, and she knew every single thing that passed across her husband's mind—literally. After thiry years, I was near the end.

"Tell me how she does it," I suggested.

He only laughed hollowly. "If I knew that would I have gone to a doctor?"

"But explain yourself. *Blanks out.* How?"

"I honestly don't know, Mr. Evans. I suppose there is a—— I *know* there is a logical explanation. I'm not superstitious, a believer in black magic and such nonsense. Some of the things we do and have done in the laboratory would startle a layman out of his senses, but behind every phenomena there is an orderly procession of facts." He sighed. "Mr. Evans, I only wish I could understand such an effect."

"How did you discover this . . . uh, effect?"

"It was just after she moved out of the house. I tried to see her, to talk things over, to ask her to come back. She left orders not to admit me and refused my phone calls. I began following her but she soon discovered me, and when she did, she simply blanked out."

"You mean . . . vanished?"

He nodded in despair. "Vanished—in mid-air, in the middle of the sidewalk, not half a block ahead of me. She didn't so much as turn around to look at me, to see If I was there. She *knew* I was there—and disappeared."

"Doorways?"

"No, I thought of that; I've thought of a hundred things. Who wouldn't when the unexplainable happens? No, it was not a doorway. In the middle of the sidewalk, I told you. It happened time and time again, crossing a street, sitting on a park bench, oh, just anywhere." He looked at me helplessly.

"How many times?" I wanted to know.

"Six, maybe seven. Then I visited my doctor, and the psychiatrist, and then I came to you because now I never see her at all. I've waited outside her hotel until I'm afraid of the patrolman on the beat, but she never, never allows me to see her any more."

I got down to business.

"In exact words, Mr. Jackson, what do you want me to do?"

"Find her! *See* her. Talk to her. Tell her I . . . I *must* see her again. Just once more."

I didn't like that last answer. "You want me to attempt a reconciliation?" I questioned.

He fell over himself in eager assent—in words. But he was a little too eager for my peace of mind.

"If not," I said, "then arrange a divorce?"

"Oh, no, no, Mr. Evans. Never that. I would never divorce Marie. I tell you, I love her, Mr. Evans."

That wasn't all of his complaint by any means, that was only the curtain raiser. Arthur Jackson spent a full two hours in my office that afternoon, crying on my shoulder. He told me his wife had always been a remarkable woman, that she was extraordinarily intelligent, and that her mind was so keen as to grasp whole problems before the verbal recital of the initial facts was fully presented.

"I can't keep anything from her!" he cried once, and went on to explain. She knew everything he knew, and more. She could fill his job or the jobs of any of his superiors, and that, to Arthur Jackson, was frightening because he was working on the most secret of government projects.

I thought I understood; he was unable to continue living with her and yet he lacked the will to give her up. One doesn't so easily part with a prize, even though that prize becomes increasingly hard to understand and manage. Could a moron mate with a savant, even when the moron was a brilliant atomic specialist in his own right?

Arthur Jackson had been an engineer in the Manhattan Project since the summer of 1940. He had also acquired a wife in the summer of 1940, although if he but realized the truth, the wife had acquired him. He now lived in Nashville and divided his time between his home here, and Oak Ridge.

Nashville was as close as *I* could get to Oak Ridge without raising suspicion. Of what earthly use were private detectives in a city like Oak Ridge, private detectives whose backgrounds could not stand investigation?

Long before that two-hour interview with Jackson had ended I learned a pair of startling facts from him, although he never mentioned either of them aloud. He had aroused my suspicions concerning his wife, to be sure, suspicions which caused me to speculate on what Brigham had told me those many years ago in Washington. But they were as nothing compared to these solid facts.

Jackson tried to guard his mind during our conversation, not from me, as I knew he did not suspect me, but from force of habit from spending ten years with his wife. It was futile. He had kept no secrets from his wife and he kept none from me.

I learned first that Marie Jackson possessed a machine in a suitcase. Jackson thought of it that way because he had never been allowed more than a glimpse of it. To him it was just a gray, shapeless mass of machinery which fitted into a suitcase that was always locked. For years he had been curious about that little machine, and now, suddenly I was too.

Secondly, I learned from him that the United States had begun research on a hydrogen bomb out there at Oak Ridge long before public announcements were made that the government was merely considering it. This was a subtle bit of strategy in itself. The first actual bomb was near completion while Congress was still debating on whether the nation should start research on it!

Arthur Jackson was key man on the project.

The shock of that nearly showed on my face, but the man before me was too overwrought to see my face. He was still protesting his undying love for his wife.

Like hell you do! You're lying, Arthur Jackson, and you don't love her—not any more, you don't. Fear has got you by the heart and jealousy by the guts. Hatred is tearing your fine intelligence right out of your skull. Your wife has left you behind like a ship sailing from a pier, and if you ever get Marie Jackson in your gunsight, you're a widower.

"All right," I said aloud, "I'll take the case. I'll try to find Mrs. Jackson for you."

The relief and gratitude on his face and in his mind was a physical thing. "I knew you would," he cut loose on me. "The paper said you were a miracle man; they said you could find absolutely anybody; they said——"

I cut him short. "A lot of eyewash. I happen to be as far advanced in my field as you are in yours. The newspaper writers add the fancy touches."

"But you *do* have a remarkable record."

"I do. And doubtless you do too. If you'll leave your address and telephone number with the girl, I'll have something to report in a few days. The retainer fee is thirty dollars."

He left. And in a short while I closed my office.

I spotted Marie Jackson in the hotel lobby.

I felt old and tired, washed up, like a horse put to pasture or a general put on the pension list. It was almost finished—my thirty-year job was as good as done. There remained only the necessary steps to close the case: make absolutely sure the woman was the one I had been seeking, and after that to mail in my report, and the job was ended. I would be on my own.

Marie Jackson came out of the elevator dressed for the street. She was a knock-out! Tall, as beautiful as a storybook queen, magnificent breasts and long, striking legs. She paused by the lobby newsstand, but didn't look at the papers. Dusk had fallen. Marie Jackson was searching the sidewalk outside the hotel for her husband. He wasn't there of course as he was at home waiting for my call. She seemed surprised at his absence and walked out regally through the door which was held open for her. Without a glance she struck off down the street.

I followed her, marvelling that a jealous husband had put

me on the trial, but I still had that empty feeling now that the trail was nearly ended.

We hadn't gone many blocks through the brightly lighted district before I stumbled onto something else, something that I had been half-expecting. Her husband had put it in a very literal way. He had said: "She sucks my mind of knowledge like a bat sucks blood." Marie Jackson was doing that now. She reached out to touch the minds of those around her seeking knowledge.

Sometimes she paused here and there, not long and not often, to sweep across their minds like my eyes swept her attractive figure.

She kept this up for the better part of three hours, going up and down streets, in and out of the park, on crowded busses, in a theater lobby, always searching, touching briefly and going on. She was finding nothing she didn't already know. I finally got tired of it and I had what I wanted for my report.

We passed a drugstore which had a pay phone. I went in and called Arthur Jackson.

"Did you find her?" he cried out immediately. "What did she say? Will she come back?" Can I see her?"

"Hold on a minute," I choked him off. "I've found her, yes, but I haven't caught up with her yet. I must see her do this 'blank-out' act, and then I'll close in. You've got to help me."

He was all eagerness to help.

"Get a cab," I instructed him. "Cruise down Charlotte Avenue past those two theaters. She's mixing with the crowd. I want you to think of her—I said *think*. Think hard. Think about finding her there on the street. She'll know you're coming, and she'll get away from the crowd. When she's in a safe place she'll pull the act. I'll be watching."

He agreed, and I left the drugstore. A minute or so later and I would have run into her as I came out the door. She had turned and was coming back along the block. I struck out ahead of her, letting her follow me. I saw to it that she did *not* touch my thoughts.

This should be interesting. I hoped that Marie Jackson wouldn't disappoint me now that the chase was at an end, hoped she was fast enough to protect herself. I couldn't afford to have anything happen to her now, couldn't let that silly ass of a husband put an end to her. The Cro-

Magnon men in their age had taken adequate care of the Neanderthal, yes, but wasn't it safe to assume that every once in a while the brute force struck first, and fatally?

I came to the mouth of an alley and paused. The alley was fairly dark and was deserted except for a pair of scavenger cats midway down. A large telephone pole, which held some kind of transformer in a locked, square case, promised sanctuary. I slid into the alley and lodged myself behind the pole, and waited.

Marie Jackson passed the mouth of the alley, still continuing her search. A part of her consciousness flicked past me, touched the cats briefly, evoking a snarling yowl. She passed from sight but I kept a careful contact, alert to flash a warning if she somehow missed her oncoming husband. She didn't. It was a distinct pleasure to watch her glide into action.

While Arthur Jackson's cab was still three minutes away she caught his thought. She also saw he packed a gun.

She suddenly stopped, glanced casually around, and again saw the mouth of the alley. Retracing her steps without visible hurry she gained the alley and turned into its concealing darkness. Then she did it. . . . disappeared! . . . "blanked out" as her husband called it. I was the only one watching. It was smooth. I found myself wishing I knew how it was done.

I kept her spotted by her thoughts, and thus pin-pointed her against a brick wall. She was completely invisible to the naked eye, mine or any other, but she had grown foolishly careless. She failed to hide her thoughts, and in the darkness of that alleyway the mental aura stood out like a neon glow. She stood with her back to the wall and waited for her husband, concealed from him but not from me. She did not fully protect herself by all the means at her command, and the Boss would want to know that and would be surprised when my report came in.

The cab crept slowly along the street, past the mouth of the alley and moved on out of our field of view. Marie Jackson watched it quietly. Her husband was leaning out the window, searching for her among the crowds on the sidewalk. He was looking for Marie—and for me. The crazy fool was looking for me! He supposed that when he saw me, she would be not far ahead.

Damn his rotten soul, he betrayed me to the woman!

She jerked around and moved away from the wall, puzzled and alarmed at this new element. Marie stepped to the alley entrance to search, stared up and down the street seeking me. Her thoughts were a chaotic frenzy and for seconds she defeated her own purpose, trying to find me by sight alone.

Damn Arthur Jackson and his weak mind, damn that stupid moron for revealing me. She flashed after him, caught his memory and scoured it for my description. Getting that, she again searched the street for me, in vain.

It was then that she began to think, to use her brain. She stopped trying to find me by sight alone and fell back on her mental powers. I blanked my mind, thought nothing, waited to see what she might do. My instructions had been not to reveal my presence, my mission, if at all possible. If for any reason I should be caught, I was on my own and had to get out the best way I could. I either ended my search and mailed in a report, or I ended my search and was prevented from mailing in a report. Either way, my success was obviously clear.

Marie had her back to the wall, thinking, analyzing. It had finally struck home and was like a bolt of lightning to her. She suddenly realized I was not to be found among that crowd on the street, that I was somewhere else not *in sight*. I was not in sight, and yet I was there. Her husband's anxious fearful mind told her all that.

Belatedly that smashed home to her and she did what she should have been doing all along. She closed up her mind to outsiders and shut off that tell-tale glow of mental activity. She vanished from me.

I did nothing, I thought nothing. I waited motionless behind the telephone pole, concealed from her sight and from her prying mind. She could not catch me unless she caught my thought, or unless she moved deeper into the alley and came abreast of the pole. We were two invisible bodies in the darkness, two tightly wrapped minds hiding our heads from each other. I knew where I was but I no longer knew where she might be.

Then the stinking cats loused it up. I had forgotten the cats and did not realize they were so near. They had worked their way up the alley. Her unseen presence frightened them and my quite visible body behind the pole annoyed them. I offered them a tangible means of expressing their nerves, so the nearest one arched its back, hissed, then clawed at me. It might as well have flashed a light on me.

I was done unless I acted fast, and the only defense I knew was a fast offense.

Without speaking aloud, I said, "Hello, Marie."

There was no answer.

I sent another thought. "Come on out, I see you."

That did it. "You can't!" she flashed at me, and the thought revealed her position and also the fact that she was frightened . . . of me!

"Oh, but I can. You're there, against the wall."

After a short silence, she asked, "Who are you?"

Who was I? I stared at her in concealed astonishment. What the hell, did she expect me to come right out and admit the truth? Did she expect me to give myself away so readily? Yes, she apparently did, so I answered and lied to her.

"I'm another, Marie, another like yourself." I directed a pointed thought toward the starry heavens, hiding from her the false base of the thought. "From up there."

Even her responding gasp reached me on the mental line.

She was frightened, damned frightened and her reaction plainly revealed it. It puzzled me—I was the expendable who was supposed to get away from one of *them* the best way I could should I be caught, and yet she was frightened of me! It didn't make sense. I waited for her to reply.

To all inward and outward appearances I was exactly like herself. If she could walk the earth in the guise of a human, as Brigham had suspected the visitors could, then she had no reason to believe that I was not doing the same. If she could probe into minds, could skim the intelligences of earthlings, then it was quite apparent to her that I was doing the same, here and now. We had looked into each other's minds and had seen only what was open for display, so it should have followed that we were both of the same kind, both of the same origin. Yet she was scared of me.

Brigham was the boss, the man I sent my reports to. I had seen him just once when my job was explained to me. He gave me a sum of money and instructed me as to the search, only he'd supposed it would be in the form of a man and I had automatically accepted the supposition. Yet it was a woman, calling herself Marie Jackson.

"Marie . . ." I questioned.

"What do you want?"

"That was a dirty trick to play on your husband."

She said again, "Who are you?"

"My name is Evans," I said patiently, and quickly covered up with, "Here on this world I am called Evans. And you are Marie Jackson."

"What are you going to do?" she asked fearfully, and I realized something else that she had attempted to hide, but failed. She really meant, what was I going to do *to her!* Me! An ordinary mortal watchdog, endowed with only one superhuman power, *telepathy.* And now that I had caught an other-worldly visitor, one of the suspected interlopers from a neighboring planet, what was *I* going to do to *her?* I'm damned if it made sense.

I slipped, I let my mind-shield loosen without my realizing it, and I thought to myself, I wish Brigham were here.

"Brigham!" she cried out instantly.

I tightened up again, instantly alert. She knew his name all right. The familiarity was in her tone and mind.

"What about Brigham?" I demanded.

"Do you . . . do you know him?"

"Yes," I admitted cautiously.

"Brigham," she persisted, "in Washington? Gray hair, left ear partly torn away? Brigham, who offered a job——?"

"Jehosophat!" I was astounded. "Not you too?"

She stepped away from the wall, the fear vanishing. "Yes. Are you one of Brigham's agents, too?"

And there it was. In the next few seconds in that dark alley, while the betraying cats scuttled away to safety, the beginning of it came out. We were both working for the same man, both watching for the same thing, and each of us had mistaken the other for an alien.

It was a ridiculous situation and yet had apparently come about because Brigham simply followed secret government procedure when hiring his agents, and had not informed either one there was already another in the field. I asked her if she wanted a drink, which she did, and we left the alley.

We were sitting in a small, cozy booth in the darkened rear of a cocktail lounge, a place well away from the theater district. Now, of all times, we had no desire for her husband to find us.

"Why did you marry him?" I asked her.

"Why, to keep watch, of course." She frowned. "Where else but near his laboratories would *they* be found?"

"I've never found one yet," I admitted.

"Nor have I. Do you suppose we ever shall?"

I shrugged. "Brigham thinks so, and there is every evidence of it. Especially since the papers began reporting these 'flying saucers.' If Brigham is right, sooner or later one of those aliens will turn up in a vital spot and we'll have him."

"I don't like it," she replied, and lapsed into telepathy. The place was noisy despite its quiet location. "I accepted the job because it seemed the best thing to do, but I don't like it. It frightens me."

I sought her hand, and held it.

"It's funny," I said, "how Brigham tried to make me believe he was an individual, hiring me on his own initiative and out of his own pocket, just to investigate a pet theory of his."

"I caught that, too!" Marie answered. "And all the time I glimpsed in his mind just who was putting up the money, who was actually beginning the investigation. Do you suppose he forgot we could read his mind?"

"One of those idiotic lapses," I laughed. Thirty years ago Brigham had put the proposition up to me and asked me if I wanted the job. He was, he claimed, just an old man who held the fantastic notion that beings from other planets were visiting Earth—he offered the books of Charles Fort as partial proof, and offered a pile of other, unpublished evidence as the remainder of the proof. He asked me to look upon him as a scientist who was conducting a laboratory experiment, asked me to search the Earth for proof. If I found such proof then his theory was proven.

He gave me a sum of money, which he said was all he could afford, and a postal address to which I was to make monthly reports. The reports in themselves were to be simple things, and so for thirty years I had been mailing one letter a month, a letter which contained but one word: "No." I had faithfully carried out his mission, because I saw behind his words, behind his carefully fabricated story about it being an old man's whim.

Brigham was a secret presidential agent.

I saw past Brigham as he talked. Behind him I saw a thoroughly alarmed president and a cabinet member, and a third party who was partly visible as a secret service agent. I saw that the money for my investigation had come from a private and confidential fund maintained by the president and accountable to no one but him. When I had looked into Brigham's mind and realized that all four of them took the interplanetary threat seriously, I began to believe. I accepted the job, I listened to the instructions, I took the money and left Brigham's house, and I've been reporting to someone ever since.

The president had died, long ago, back near the beginning of my thirty-year task. The cabinet member was shuffled somewhere into the discard and I had no idea where he might be now. I had not been back to see Brigham, and did not know if Brigham still personally directed the search or if he too had died and another was carrying on in his place. Brigham had still been there ten years ago when Marie came, when she married Arthur Jackson and settled down near the Manhattan Project. Brigham might still be there for all either of us knew.

Meanwhile I had grown up in the job, had come to believe in it completely, and was constantly on the alert for evidence that an alien walked the Earth, that someone or something from the nearer planets was among us, watching and waiting. Waiting for the birth of interplanetary travel, in all likelihood.

We sat there, Marie and I, comparing notes. It was curious the way her own progress was comparable to mine. She knew no more of Brigham and the people behind him than I did, had no other memories of him different than my own. She knew as much—or as little—about the entire picture as I knew, and could add no original touch of her own. Her job, she told me, had come to her in the exact manner as mine had.

Marie's warm and lovely body was touching mine, and with a detached corner of my mind I envied those years Arthur Jackson had lived with her. There was really no sane reason to envy the past, I told myself. Marie was mine, now. Jackson had wanted an equal as a mate, someone who matched his own intelligence. Until now, this moment, I had been certain I'd never find my mate—for where else on Earth lived another telepath? Suddenly I felt an outside warmth stealing over me, and realized for the first time how a mental blush might feel. I stared at the girl. The blush was sweeping into her cheeks.

"Sorry," I apologized. "I'll have to learn to keep such thoughts to myself."

She smiled but didn't answer. I dropped deeper into my mental state to spare her further embarrassment, and thought about her. From the corner of my eye I noted the bewitching breasts jutting up through her dress, the lean ripeness of her body and its more apparent compliment, the lovely face.

No wonder her husband was madly in love with her, no wonder he desired to possess that body, and no wonder he nearly went mad when that beautiful wife disappeared from him, "blanked-out" her loveliness.

Blanked-out!

I sat up, stunned. What a sucker I had been!

Marie Jackson, a Brigham agent—like hell! She knew no more about Brigham than I did, had no other memory of him than my own. Of course she didn't, she knew no more of him than she had read in my own mind. From the time I had dropped my barrier in that alley and let Brigham's name slip through she had been using my own thoughts to deceive me! Had even tried to make me forget the one startling, paramount difference between us: she could vanish at will! I could not.

I had been right the first time. Marie was an alien.

"Jehosophat!" I said suddenly, pulling away from her. "Your husband!"

"Where?" She jumped.

"Not here—I didn't mean that," I said hastily, "but I forgot to call him back. I'm supposed to report on you, and we certainly don't want him to come walking in here. I'll call now."

"Must you, *now?*" she asked softly with words, and sending along with them a suggestive undertone of thought.

"I don't want to, believe me. I want to stay right here with you until hell freezes over." I carefully hid the lie and forced myself to return an intimate thought. "The sooner we get him out of the way, the sooner you and I—" and I let the suggestion hang there.

She smiled lazily. I got out of the booth and signalled the waiter for another round of drinks. She said, "Please don't be too long."

"Count on me," I replied. I looked again at her striking features and once more envied Arthur Jackson in his ignorance.

She winked and I walked over to the telephone booths. As soon as I was out of her line of sight I closed off from her my flow of thought and got the devil out of there, out the back way and down the street as fast as my feet would carry me. People stared at me as I ran. Marie was deadly. I wanted to get as much distance between us as was possible.

I ran until I found an empty cab and jumped in. "Get moving fast!" I snapped at the driver. I gave him the address of Arthur Jackson's home, hoping the man had given up the street search for us and returned there.

Marie Jackson—the thing I had been set to catch, had very neatly caught me.

I wanted to warn Jackson first because his danger was immediate, and because I did owe him a certain loyalty . . . he was a human being. And when I reported to Brigham I would not tell him how I had been taken in, would not tell him she had pretended to be another searcher like myself, that she had hoodwinked me with a feigned fright and pretended fear of me. She had lied to me, tricked me with word and thought, cleverly followed my conversational line on my search with insertions of her own which sounded as if she, too, had known Brigham. I didn't want him to know I had fallen flat on my face.

By using some sort of tremendous mental power which an earthborn telepath—myself—did not have and could not guess at, she had vanished from sight. She was from the *outside,* from up there where humans hoped to be someday.

The cab pulled up in front of Arthur Jackson's house. The lighted windows in one of the rooms told me where he was.

I dashed across the lawn and stopped in midflight, astonished. That which came spilling across the wide yard with the light told me something else. Marie was ahead of me.

"You want to kill me!" came the mental image of his accusation.

"You are a fool," she snapped. "This job is ended."

I hastily circled the house, searching the windows, and found a set of screened kitchen-windows open to the night. I crawled up through one of them, and lowered myself to the kitchen floor without a sound, and started quietly through the darkness of the house toward the lighted room. My mind caught a sense of urgency from Marie. I paused, sought out ahead of me and found she was working on a metallic object. She was not expecting me yet.

Her husband was frightened, and confused as to her presence and her purposes, and in his ignorant fear he was babbling furiously without pausing to organize his words. I listened to them for only a second and turned my attention back to his wife. Marie was extremely busy on *something* and I could pick up only bits of her concentrated thought. She was hurriedly attempting to take a fix upon some object which had moved, or to arrange a fix upon it. The fragments of concentration were very vague.

I crept closer to the lighted doorway, moved along until Arthur Jackson came into view. He was seated in a chair, held there by visible bonds, staring at her and talking. I listened to him again.

". . . kill me, you found out what you wanted to know and you're going to kill me, you found out about the project and you're going to radio your friends, you're a spy but don't think I haven't been wise to you because I have, and I hired a man to follow you, so if you kill me now . . ."

He went on and on but I had lost interest in what he was saying. He had said radio. Radio—the machine in the suitcase, which earlier that day I had glimpsed in his mind, the thing on which his wife was now working. Marie Jackson was setting up a fix to find a position which had moved, and her husband thought it was a radio.

I remembered his earlier words, his telling me that he discovered her reading a schematic. I knew then what she was doing, what she was working on. With that key to her vague mental pattern, I could assemble the spillage that came my way and see what she was doing.

He thought it was a radio, thought she was using it to relay information on the hydrogen bomb back to her countrymen in Europe. He was only partly right. Marie Jackson was setting up a fix on her home planet, a body which had moved in space since she last used the instrument. The machine was the only kind of a communicator which was capable of piercing the Heaviside Layer, a combination telepathic-electronic transmitter which broadcast on a tight beam to a fixed position. It was a transmitter which employed an electrically stepped-up mental force to hurl a message across space to another planet.

She suddenly ceased working. I froze against the wall, waiting to see if she had discovered me but no thought from her indicated that. Instead she put out a feeler toward the street, splayed the mental search beam over a wide area seeking my presence. Satisfied that I had not yet approached the house, she dropped it.

The work on the transmitter was finished. Jackson was still babbling.

In a flaring instant of anger she silenced him, hurled a mental force which paralyzed his tongue, and the man fell dumb, choking. I carefully followed that, and noticed that she had also paralyzed his legs. That was why he had never left the chair since I had come into the house. Marie walked around a table nearer to him.

"Arthur," she said aloud, slowly, so that he would understand, "you're a fool! The man you hired to follow me is a fool!"

I remained motionless in the darkness, against the wall. I listened to her words with my ears, but my mind was reaching out to that instrument, examining it, studying the manner of its operation, looking for the inlet which received the mental thought and amplified it.

"I have little choice in the matter," she was saying. "If I allow you to continue your work on that unit you call a 'hydrogen bomb' I will be hastening the death of my own world. You do not know it but your military forces are as far advanced on space rockets as you are on this 'bomb' unit. Do you see what that means?

"Do you see what little choice I have? Arthur Jackson, we cannot allow your race to get off this planet for you are much too dangerous, too deadly! You are not yet fit to leave your planet for you would only spread your blackness to mine, to the other worlds. And so you must stay here until your race has conquered its own murderous habits.

"I am sorry, Arthur Jackson, but you must die, and any other man who follows in your place must die—until the time comes when your race can be trusted. The only other alternative is to eliminate this planet completely—to bring about an accident in your experimental laboratories, to cause this 'hydrogen bomb' weapon to turn upon its makers. Surely you do not want that, nor do we. But your work must be stopped, and to stop that it is necessary to stop you——"

She stopped then in mid-sentence and whirled in alarm. Behind her the transmitter had flared into life.

In two short seconds it was over and she was too late. I

had found the input channel, found the way to activate the mechanism. It was that which had caused her alarm. As she whirled to stare at it, I stepped through the doorway.

Using her own words, coldly, without emotion, I thought into the transmitter: "The job is ended."

The lost two seconds were her undoing. Once before on that evening she had betrayed a fatal weakness, revealed her inability to make split-second decisions and act on them. Marie had spent too many years on Earth and had grown careless of her training. She made the second mistake I knew she would make.

She started for the machine instead of hurling a contradictory thought into it, instead of jamming the transmission of my message by forcing one of her own. I dived for the table where the transmitter lay.

She reached it first, bent over it, and I chopped my hand down on the back of her neck.

I swear to God I didn't know that would kill her.

It wouldn't have killed a human—there was not that much force behind it. I had forgotten—or perhaps the fact never so much as occurred to me—that she wasn't human.

Marie Jackson was dead, and in her death she was changed. The mental image she had built around herself to walk Earth unnoticed was fading as fast as her mind died. The guise of a woman she had long ago assumed was slipping away and I did not like what was left. I stepped over the body, turned to her husband in the chair.

Arthur Jackson was dead, strangled to death on his own paralyzed tongue. I stood there a moment looking at him, wondering if he had lived long enough to see what his "wife" really looked like.

And then I walked out of the room into the little entrance hall which contained a telephone. Standing there in the semi-darkness, I dialed the Western Union number.

"I want to send a night letter," I said to the clerk, and gave him Brigham's name and the post box number in Washington.

"And the message, sir?"

"Just say: 'The job is ended.'"

I confess to being addicted to time travel tales. I have written several of them, have read perhaps a hundred of them, but yet I cannot get enough. A writer (and the reader too, for that matter) can construct wonderfully crazy, convoluted twists of plot and sanity if he has a trusty time machine to hand, and never mind that sophomoric business of traveling backward in time to kill your own grandfather. Give some thought to journeying forward to bump off your own grandson before *he* does you in.

With my trusty time machine at hand, I would journey back to the early years of this century to teach a young, destitute writer how to operate the machine. He would be both pleased and surprised—mostly surprised.

ABLE TO ZEBRA

HORACE REID KICKED ASIDE THE THOROUGHLY scanned copy of the New York *Times* and finished the last of the coffee in his breakfast cup. With no real interest he reached for the San Francisco *Chronicle* and lazily thumbed through its pages. Both of the papers were a day old and he had known the news they contained twenty-four hours ago, while it was still fresh, but still it was his daily chore to read those and the others littering the floor. Situated at the opposite ends of the country as those two were, they might contain some small item of purely local interest that his own Chicago papers would never know.

The important national news came over the radio of course. Listening to that too, was a weary chore. But it was the occasional regional story that needed his attention.

Horace dropped the *Chronicle* after awhile and reached for the coffee percolator. Empty. He looked over the table, found nothing more to eat other than the broken crusts of the toast, and resigned himself. Carefully lighting a cigarette, he reached for the morning *Tribune*.

The matter was on page eight.

Horace studied the story slowly at first, after working his way through the headline; he supposed he would never get used to the tight, compact, and not always sensible combination of words the headline writers here employed to gain attention.

PROF DENIES INDIANS SWAPPED WAMPUM FOR PENNIES

Digesting that with but a second's hesitation he grasped the headline's message: some professor had denied that native aborigines exchanged their money for that of others. So? That was worth a headline? He swept on into the body of the story and was abruptly jerked to attention.

According to the brief dispatch, filed by AP from a small Illinois river town the preceding evening, a Professor Forrestor of State Normal University and his class of archeology students had unearthed a new Indian mound along the banks of the Illinois, one of many that had been located in the region. Other than the normal student excitement over the find, the opening and preparing of the mound had followed in the usual manner. A number of skeletons were uncovered, along with their paraphernalia: weapons, beads, pottery and trinkets. In one corner of the mound the definitely unusual turned up. The skeleton of a one-armed Indian was located, with that one bony arm wrapped possessively around a glass jar full of Indian-head pennies.

Horace stopped reading to consider that.

"By George!" he said. And then he giggled.

Old Forrestor at first believed he was the victim of a student hoax, a belief shared by a Mr. Jay Toliver, official representative of the state archeology society who was attached to the class on this field trip. Following an emphatic denial by the students, a minute examination of the find "proved" that no hoax was involved. Both Forrestor and Toliver agreed in declaring that the mound and its complete contents were of equal antiquity; the one-armed Indian and his strange treasure had been buried together about 400 years ago. Officials of the state and experts at the University of Illinois were hurrying to the scene.

Horace said "By George!" once more, and dropped the newspaper. The giggle spread across his face in a wide grin and soon he was laughing aloud.

From his bookshelf he pulled a large volume, leafing through it until he found a relief map of the state; after that he put in a long distance telephone call to the chief of police in the river town. Posing as a reporter for a radio wire service, he queried the policeman on the previous night's discovery and on recent developments since then. There were no new developments, he learned, except that carloads of people had arrived from the state capitol, the university, and every other city and town within a hundred mile radius to examine and gawk at the uncovered mound. It was creating quite a traffic problem, the chief declared. The mound itself? No, nothing new there—the experts still wrangled.

Horace thanked him and hung up. Carefully removing all traces of amusement from his voice and thoughts, he placed the palm of his hand close to his partly opened mouth and blew a hot breath on it, activating the metal plate beneath the skin. Presently there was a queer ringing in his ears.

"Zebra," he said to the palm. "Location: Love."

"Able here," the voice of a tired old man said in his ear. "Yes?"

Horace stifled an inner thrill. He had never spoken to Able before, had never made contact with anyone that highly placed in official circles. After all, Zebra was on the lowest rung of the seniority list and he seldom had the opportunity to know the really top persons and places. Able himself!

"I have to report an anachronism, sir."

"Oh my stars!" the old man said. "Another one? Your location is Love, did you say?"

"Yes, sir. I'm on change of duty, sir. I understand some-one else is filling my former position on—"

"I know, I know all that!" Able interrupted testily. "I sent the substitute to Zebra myself. Very well, what is this one? And don't tell me its another magnetic motor!"

Horace took a deep breath. "No, sir. There haven't been any more of those since Hendershot in 1928. This is quite different. A university class opened a mass grave of native aborigines last evening, sir. They found in the grave a glass jar containing coins minted some 400 years later. The coins bore the images of those same aborigines, by peculiar co-incidence, and were minted by the present-day government as a sort of token to them."

"Oh my, oh my, oh my," Able's tired voice ejaculated. "This is worse than I thought, this is much worse than the motors. Oh, this is dreadful!" He paused for a long mo-ment and Horace could almost picture the old man ponder-ously shaking his head. "Tch, tch, tch. What is your exact location and date?"

"Chicago, Illinois," Horace told him, and added the street address. He shot a quick glance at the morning pa-per. "Wednesday, July 9, 1952."

"Oh my stars," Able repeated. "I'll have to send you as-sistance at once."

"Will that be necessary sir?" Horace broke in boldly. "I realize that I'm new here, but I'd like the chance to prove my—"

"No, no, positively no," the old one cut him off. "Out of

the question young man—no reflection on your able judgment intended. This is far more serious than you may realize, far more serious indeed. That present government of yours . . . tch, tch. Who can I send you?"

Horace waited, not daring to suggest. Vaguely in his ear he heard the ancient one running down the list of his operatives' code names. "Able, Baker, Charlie, Dog, Easy, Fox . . ." The cosmic leader paused briefly over Fox, considering that worthy for a moment before continuing his low rumble. Suddenly he raised his voice with decision. "I'll send you either Charlie or Dog . . . must look to see who is free right now. Make no move until arrival."

"Yes, sir," Horace said with concealed disappointment.

"Out," Able said wearily. "Oh, my. . . ."

Horace dropped his hand to his lap, vaguely annoyed with the old one. He couldn't disobey his superior, but this was *such* a perfect opportunity to display his talents. Really the first opportunity he'd had, for his own little world was a dull place—nothing ever happened there. Perhaps if he—

Horace seized the phone book, searching for the addresses of the nearest library and a costumer's shop. He could at least lay the groundwork for a scheme shaping up in his mind, could at least *hope* to interest Charlie or Dog in the scheme. For a long moment he contemplated the newspapers on the floor and then he giggled once more. "I think it rather funny," he said to his apartment walls. "Just imagine, Indian-head pennies . . ."

Bottom-rung agent Zebra, alias Horace Reid in Chicago, lazily pushed himself up on the oversized bed and stretched. Another day, another stack of the native newspapers to go through, another struggle with the cryptic headlines, and another three or four meals of the delicious Love variety. The newspapers might not always make sense but the planet Love provided him with the most tempting, satisfying food he had ever known. His own little world of Zebra, a primitive and volcanic mudball, had nothing to compare with the edibles of Love.

Why, he wondered next, had Operative Love ever left Love, causing him, Zebra, to vacate Zebra and patrol Love during the man's absence? He moved over to the edge of the bed and dangled a bare foot. Code names were all right in their place, too, but it tended to be confusing when the overseer of a planet temporarily left the place. To make it all simpler, why didn't Able patrol his Able, Baker take care of Baker, and so on down the line to Zebra on Zebra, with special trouble-shooters coming in during these emergencies? But no—that wasn't such a happy thought either. In that event he, Zebra, wouldn't have discovered the wonderful cookery of Love.

And returning to primitive Zebra after this tour of duty would be like returning to work after a very pleasant vacation.

Horace sighed and slipped out of bed to pad across the room in bare feet, liking the sounds his feet made on the floor. Pushing open the swinging door to the kitchenette, he stopped stockstill to stare at the blonde.

Primitive Zebra had no blondes like *that,* either!

She glanced up quickly from the small white stove and smiled at him, a beautiful thing to receive so early in the morning. "Good morning, Zebra. You're a late sleeper."

Horace brightened. "Charlie, sir?" he asked hopefully. This was wonderful, this was unexpected! To awaken and find a ravishing blonde person in one's kitchenette was an unusual treat—even though the blond was one's superior officer. So *she* was to work with him on the case!

The girl shook her head. "Dog."

Zebra-Horace considered that doubtfully. She was, in the current vernacular, a cute trick, a rare dish, even though she held considerable seniority over him and he must remember to be properly deferential. He said respectfully, "We'll have to give you a new name here, sir. Chicago, 1952, might not appreciate a blonde dog."

"Agreed." She smiled that rare smile once more and continued the preparation of breakfast. "What name are you using here?"

"Horace Reid."

"Then I had best be Mrs. Horace Reid." There was a little more than just casual amusement in her voice. "I'll be staying here, and your people will talk."

"Yes, sir."

She indicated the meal on the stove and then motioned to him. "This is almost ready. Why not put on some clothes?"

Horace looked down at himself and ran for the bedroom.

Dog proved herself a remarkable cook. Working through the breakfast with appreciation and relish, Horace glanced up at her as the quick thought struck him.

"You've been here before."

"Briefly." She nodded the attractive golden head across the table. "During one of the earlier wars—something about tea and taxes, I believe." Her lovely brown eyes rested seriously on his face. "Don't let yourself like it too well. You can't stay."

"I can't help it," Zebra confessed. "You are a wonderful cook. Sir."

The girl abruptly switched the subject. "Tell me about your problem. Able was very upset, and very sketchy."

He outlined it to her while they ate, explaining the ancient customs among these particular aborigines of mass burial, together with their favorite weapons, their treasures and personal charms and omens. Today, certain sciences had advanced to the point where individuals and groups were now actively seeking and opening these burial mounds for study purposes. The grave opened two days before had contained, in addition to the usual accouterments, a most perplexing anachronism, a glass jar filled with coins minted by the present government some four centuries after the burial. This particular jar was found in such a position and condition that responsible authorities at the site were forced to only one conclusion: Indian and money had been buried together. The morning news reports—he indicated the papers on the floor—could shed no further light on the discovery. Most scientific authorities were taking a serious and puzzled view of the situation, and some government agents were already en route from the nation's capitol to examine the find, to study the coins for authenticity.

Dog shook her golden head. "That *is* bad. Quite obviously we can't substitute counterfeit coins, for that, too, would be anachronistic. What about the students?"

"Too late," Zebra-Horace answered. "If I could have reached one of them immediately after the opening of the grave, I could have arranged a hoax. But it is far too late now. The students are adamant—and just as puzzled."

"No wonder the old one was so upset." Dog drummed her fingers on the tabletop. "Do you suppose we can erect an ancient tunnel beneath the site? Arrange it so that the jar of money was brought into the tunnel and placed in the grave from below, merely as a hiding place?"

"No, sir, not there. The terrain and the nearby river forbid it. And too, I suspect that the external evidence on the jar proves its equal age, else the scientists involved would have by now passed it off as hoax or accident."

When she didn't answer, he continued.

"It's a peculiar type of humor involved, sir. These aborigines are called Indians by the present populace, and the coins are known as Indian-head pennies because they bear the image of an Indian. Do you appreciate that?"

"I appreciate it," she told him dryly. "But wait until you advance—you'll find some you won't think so humorous."

Zebra felt as though he had been set back in his place, forcibly reminded of his lower seniority and lack of cosmic experience. He said quietly, "Yes, sir."

"Don't sir me. The name is Dog." She smiled to take away the sting. "There aren't so many of the anachronisms left anymore—we've done a fair job of weeding them out. But still, now and then one turns up such as this and we have a job on our hands. Some of them are humorous, some are cruel, some subtle. Frankly, the latter aren't so difficult to dispose of; often they are *so* subtle as to defeat their own purpose and we are able to remove them before the truth is realized. The cruel and the humorous give us more trouble."

Horace nodded sympathetically. "Children are like that —sometimes cruel, sometimes subtle, sometimes deadly in an innocent way."

"They are," she agreed. "And if we had recognized that fact earlier and watched them more closely, superintended their every idle hour as well as their training periods, all this wouldn't be necessary. That particular group of errant boys wouldn't have caused this mischief, wouldn't have made it necessary to set up a constant watch of the 26 worlds to undo their misdeeds." Dog waved a slim hand toward the morning sunlight spilling in the window. "You will notice they seemed to concentrate on this neighborhood."

"I haven't found anything on Zebra," Zebra told her. "Not in all the years I've been there."

"They probably never strayed that far—the teachers missed them early and did a quick job of rounding them up. Most of the troubles have appeared *here*, and in three or four other worlds. King had a bad time a few years ago."

"King?" Horace-Zebra questioned. "Oh yes—he's on the one with a dark star. King."

"The boys introduced sun dials on King. Poor King had an awful time rounding them up and explaining them away. Well—" she shrugged and made as if to push back from the table. "It can't happen again, and when we have finally erased the last anachronism, found and eliminated the last hybrid, the last childish joke, our job is over. So let us concentrate on the immediate problem. The hoax and tunnel angles are eliminated—have you thought of any other possible solutions?"

"Yes, sir," he told her eagerly. "I tried to interest Able, but he . . . Well sir, I favor a time machine explanation."

"*No*. Absolutely not!" Dog stood up too quickly and her chair toppled backward. "This planet does not have and will never have time machines, thank *Mechob* for small favors! Time machines are foreign to this world, unheard of —the people haven't so much as dreamed of them. You shall not introduce them as the solution!"

"Oh, no." Horace protested quickly. He left the table and hurried around to her. "I wan't thinking of their *introduction,* sir, only the suggestion of same. A mere suspicion that they *might* exist. You see, sir, a peculiar situation exists here, one very ripe for exploitation. I feel sure we can use it to our advantage and sow suspicion. There is a phenomenon on this planet known as *science fiction magazines*. The natives are positively crazy about them. They publish incredible fantasy and science romances, wild adventure yarns of the prehistoric past, even wilder tales of the probable future. They print—" he broke off in frustrated eagerness.

"Please, sir . . . come with me. These science fiction things defy description. You *have* to see them to believe them." He was gently tugging on her arm.

"Well . . ." Dog hesitated, searching his face. "You really think we can use them? Where is this—"

"Just down the block, sir. A book and magazine store." Zebra hesitated with a sudden bashfulness. "And, sir, I think perhaps you had best slip something over your shoulders." He carefully avoided a direct stare at her bare poitrine. "I may have something in the wardrobe . . . Chicago 1952, er . . . uh. . . ."

Zebra led her gaily down the stairs of the apartment building and out onto the street, both of them blinking against the bright summer sun. Together they walked to the corner, skillfully avoiding caroming children on roller skates, to cross the intersection and continue down another street. Eagerly, Zebra pointed to a small sign swaying in the gentle breeze.

"There, see . . . Mahaffey's Rocket Shop. It is run by a young lady who formerly edited a science fiction magazine; she made a fortune and retired, to open this book store. Just wait until you see these things!"

"I wish I could share your enthusiasm," Dog said.

"The magazines are marvelous! Quite like our nursery tales, really. They constantly employ rocket ships, great inventions, fantastic battles, horrible monsters . . . anything. Nothing seems too wild for them, for their readers. And by the proper planting and use, our time machine concept *could* be made into an accepted thing here—fictionally, of course. We could so skillfully implant our idea that several writers would seize upon it, enlarge it, make it into a common device. We could cause the time machine to become as well-known as the rocket ship. And through these very magazines and books we could accomplish our misdirection."

They paused before the store and inspected a tiny display window. Zebra pointed silently to a row of magazines embellished with garish covers, and just behind them a row of books. The blonde Dog stepped closer to examine the magazine covers, glancing from one to another. Finally she looked up at her waiting companion.

"You needn't have been so concerned with my lack of clothing," she pointed out. "These women are wearing about the same."

Zebra-Horace fought away a slow blush. "These pictures merely illustrate the romances, sir. Quite typical of the fiction, and perhaps indoor family wear as well. But you mustn't be seen like that on the streets." He moved in beside her to waggle an index finger. "These are only a sampling, there are dozens more inside. The publishers have designed them to appeal to all ages and tastes—from the cradle to the grave and from the schizoid to the scholar, so to speak. Their titles are frequently indicative . . . *.44 Calibre Space Adventures* . . . *Wanton Worlds* (that cover is rather obvious, isn't it?) . . . *Universal Science Fiction.* I read that one myself; it's quite good. Shall we go inside?"

He held the door open for her, and followed her in, nodding at a young woman and a couple of boys near the back of the shop.

"That's Miss Mahaffey, the owner," he whispered. "The young males are *fans*."

"Are *what?*" Dog demanded.

"Science fiction followers—avid purchasers and readers. They read everything that is published—they and the millions like them are the ones I hope to dupe with my scheme."

Zebra and the girl stopped before a large rack of magazines. He reached for a couple, opened them at random and handed them to her. "As yet," he explained, "the time machine is unknown; you'll find no mention of such here."

"And your scheme?" she asked.

"Has two equal parts, sir; each part dependent on the other for the success of the whole. And I firmly believe that success will easily explain away the anachronism of the Indian coins.

"My plan is first to induce one of the science fiction editors to send a special correspondent to the grave site, a man having a splendid reputation in his trade and who would make a thorough, analytical study of the anachronism to finally arrive at the only acceptable answer according to his logic: a time machine."

"But there are no—"

"Please, sir, hear me out. Your objection is to the second part of my scheme, which will be taken care of. Now of course, the reserved scientific world will not believe our special correspondent—they'll laugh at him. *But* the science fiction readers, these fans will believe him! And as time goes on and no one else is able to offer an alternative theory, the correspondent's report will be more or less accepted. Thereafter, official government circles will either ignore the matter entirely, as is their wont, or they will engage in secret experiments looking toward the discovery and building of such a machine." Horace smiled. "This last would prove quite harmless, of course."

"I'm still dubious," the girl told him, glancing from the shelves to the fans loitering in the rear. "These magazines—"

"Have just about the proper historical background to fit our special needs," Horace broke in. "Let me brief you. The man or men who first published them were dreamers and visionaries beyond the norm; and in time so many of their dreams and prophecies came to pass that their fellow men took notice, thereby gaining for the magazines a small measure of fame. Some of the guesses and dreams proved remarkably accurate, you see. So accurate as to command attention. Of late, three other events have occurred which added greatly to the prestige of the publications, events giving them an added stature in the eyes of the public."

Dog listened skeptically, but in silence.

"The first of these occurrences was the application of atomic power—more properly, raw nuclear fission of low order—for war use. The magazines had long since employed such power in their pages and one renowned writer had foretold atomic bombs. The one important event however was a story which closely described a bomb-detonating mechanism, a story published at the very moment the government was developing that mechanism in secret. It was so real that government security agents were alarmed, and naturally, after the close of the war, this news leaked out and widespread publicity followed. Vast sections of the reading public turned to science fiction, seeking other things their government may have hidden from them.

"Sometime following that, several of the magazines boldly attempted to explain a series of celestial objects termed *flying saucers,* or *discs.* While the military authorities declaimed and vainly suggested mass hallucinations, the magazines scoffed at their declaimers and set about proving otherwise, by photographs, eyewitness accounts and so forth. Again the result was widespread publicity and again large masses of the lay public swung toward the magazines. Their power was becoming strongly entrenched." He dropped his voice to a whisper. "That was how Miss Mahaffey made her fortune and retired to this shop. Her magazine was one of the leaders in the flying saucer mystery."

"And the third event?" Dog asked stolidly.

"The crowning achievement," Horace told her. "It was so new and revolutionary that it raised a storm in both lay and scientific circles. Science fiction magazines, early in their lives, introduced the idea of an orbital satellite, mainly as a sort of stepping-off place for interplanetary flights but also incidentally usable for observation and military control of the planet itself. These fictional *space platforms* were seized upon by one government and intensive research was begun to build and launch such an object. Before they could do so, however, they were conquered by a second government, which promptly took over the plans and started work on a platform of their own. Of course, the magazines were quick to point out that they had originated the concept many decades before—that the governments were merely copying their ideas again. The public applauded."

"I'm beginning to see your point. But go on."

"The result of all this—after many years—is a state of undeclared war between the magazines and the governments. In some few countries the publications are forbidden altogether. In others, severe restrictions are imposed upon them. Right here, in Chicago, no magazine is permitted to reveal that the critical mass of U-235 is just 22.7 pounds; yet that figure is common knowledge over much of the world. The magazines realize they have the upper hand because their editors and authors are years ahead of the politicians; whereas the politicians and bureaucrats do their best to hamper and restrict the magazines—rather naïvely believing they still have secrets the public at large is unfit to know. Unwilling to admit that thinking men the world over know their secrets, they regard the science fiction magazines as arch-enemies for revealing them, hinting at them, employing them in fiction. Caught squarely in the middle of course is the lay public—and this very situation is the weapon to solve our case.

"The public, now realizing they are in the middle, are swinging in ever-increasing numbers toward the magazines because these publications have been *so* right in the past, with the politicians *so* wrong or untruthful. Their distrust of the politician dates back for thousands of years. In short then, sir, if we suddenly introduce the startling concept of a time machine, the local government will immediately deny it. And the public, noting that denial, will believe the magazines."

The beautiful Dog replaced the magazines she had been holding. "Is there an alternative to the time machine?" she asked doubtfully. Suddenly she pointed to a book on a nearby shelf. "What about that man, Fort? Your predecessor used him to advantage."

"Oh, *no*, sir. Fort is a different sort of proposition altogether. The man is considered by most to be a crank or a crackpot and very few place any faith in him. My predecessor *did* use him well, but in a reverse manner. For instance, upon two or three occasions some of the natives have discovered what they term *magnetic motors:* the children's toys, really—I don't know if our truants left them behind on purpose or by accident. In the previous century, public curiosity wasn't what it is today, and the first two toys didn't present so much of a problem. But on the third occasion, my predecessor arranged to have the motor exposed and its finder labeled a jokester. He also saw to it that Fort seized upon it, as well as the two earlier examples. The misdirection worked very well there. But we can't use Fort, sir, his reputation being the opposite of what we wish to accomplish here."

Dog stalked along the aisle examining the books and periodicals, her eyes resting momentarily on the titles. *The Conquest of Space, The City in the Sea, The Haploids* . . . "You believe then that the time machine explanation is best?"

"Yes, sir, I do! Knowing these people and their vivid imaginations, it seems to be the only sure solution."

"How quickly could you induce an editor to dispatch an investigator to the graves?"

"In an hour or less. We can place a man on the site this afternoon; and sir, we had best arrange to have the man release a part of his findings to tomorrow's newspapers. That will lay the groundwork and serve to establish the theory early, for the magazine itself will not be able to publish his findings for another month or two."

"Possibly you are right. I admit I can see no other solution. But wait—you said there were *two* parts. And what are you going to do about introducing the concept? I understand your solution as fas as it goes, but—"

Zebra-Horace quickly caught her arm and guided her out of the book shop. The sun was still bright in their eyes. He led the way back to his apartment, talking rapidly.

"Introducing the concept *is* the second part of my plan, sir. I've done a bit of research at the library and have found the proper time and location to implant the concept. Several years ago, a writer did a series of articles for a paper called *Science Schools Journal*. These articles—he entitled them The Chronic Argonauts—contain a germ of an idea that we can put to our own use. I propose to visit that writer, to place him in economic jeopardy. The Chronic Argonauts—and our science fiction correspondent will serve us very well." They climbed the stairway.

"I don't know," the lovely Dog replied, frowning. She waited while the man unlocked the apartment door and stood aside to let her enter. "That sounds frightfully vague. . . ."

Zebra-Horace closed the door behind him, trying to hide his anxiety. She surely wouldn't dismiss his plan of action now! He ran over to the wardrobe and brought out some costumes he had rented, crossed the room again to fling open the door to an unused room.

"Please, sir . . . trust me? I want *so* much to prove my mettle to you and Able!" The gleaming metal framework of his time machine rested in the darkness of the inner room. Boldly, Horace vaulted into the saddle and held out his two arms to her.

After a moment's hesitation, Dog allowed herself to be lifted up into his lap. Horace threw a small lever.

It was early morning, the sun not yet over the rim of buildings across the street. A cold, swirling fog hung in the air, chilling them.

"We could have been better prepared," Dog said shortly. "Is this the right place?"

"Yes, sir. This is known as Mornington Road. The man we seek lives in that rooming house across the way, with a lovely young woman who is not his wife. Their present circumstances aren't particularly pleasant. Both the writer and his lady friend are consumptive, his markets are falling off, no one seems very interested in his scientific articles, and his absent wife has presented him with a troublesome bill of divorcement. As a result, he is in a somewhat dejected mood and is considering moving to a house in the country." Horace made sure the shrubbery concealed his machine, and stepped out to explore the street. "Now. Presently he will come out in his night clothes to see what may be in the mailbox. At that moment I will approach him, and pass myself off as a visiting writer from the continent. I will instill in him the idea of rewriting The Chronic Argonauts as a scientific romance. And at this point I need your help, sir."

"My help? How?" She peered across the street at the house, annoyed with the damp fog.

Horace slipped a bit of paper into her hand. "This is the address of an editor named Henley, a good friend of our writer. Henley recently lost his magazine and is searching for financial backing to launch another. If you please, sir, I want you to journey about one week into the future and offer the financial aid the editor needs. With a new magazine in his hands, Henley is sure to request our writer for material. And in the meanwhile, I will have convinced the man to take a vacation in the country, and rewrite the articles."

"Zebra," she replied sharply, "I have heard of some fantastic schemes to explain or hide anachronisms during my career, but this one is the—" She broke off cautiously as a door opened across the street.

"Please!" Zebra-Horace implored. "Please sir . . . help me on this. This is my first big job! Go see that man Henley, and meet me back here in a few hours." He turned away from her and stepped into the street, calling across to the man in the doorway. "George! Hallo, there, George . . . is that you?"

The Chicago sun had grown quite warm and the streets were reflecting up the heat, making the city uncomfortable. Children skated more slowly if at all, preferring to lounge in the shade or spend their time in inviting doorways.

A confident Horace led the beautiful girl along the street, crossing an intersection to turn in another direction. Eagerly, he pointed to a small sign hanging motionless in the heat of day.

"Look, sir! Mahaffey's Time Capsule! Our friend's Chronic Argonauts has accomplished everything!" They paused a moment outside the store and inspected the tiny display window. Zebra pointed silently to a row of magazines embellished with garish covers, and just behind them a row of books. The blonde Dog stepped closer to examine the magazine covers, glancing from one to another. Finally she looked up at her waiting companion.

"The titles would certainly seem to indicate you are right," she conceded. "Just look at them: *Slave Goddess of the Time-Worm, Ravished in Time's Abyss, The Rape of the Time Maidens*." She shook her blonde head in wonderment. "All the writers seem to have caught the idea, Heinlein, Bradbury, Marlowe, Mudgett, Shaver, Byrdbatthe. . . ."

Zebra held the shop door open for her, followed her into the cool interior. He nodded to the young woman and a couple of boys near the back of the store.

"My plan of action must be a success, sir, and our special correspondent will visit the grave site this afternoon."

He pointed happily to a shelf of books. "See—*The Omnibus of Time, Adventures in Time and Space* . . . we have planted well!" Zebra was searching the shelves carefully, eagerly, searching for a particular title. Suddenly he reached down to snatch a slim, blue volume from its resting place. "Here it is!"

Dog turned the book around to read the legend on the spine. *"The Time Machine,* by H. G. Wells. We did this?"

"Yes, sir, this started it all. That man in the rooming house—"

Suddenly, unexpectedly, Dog kissed him full on the lips. The shop mistress and the two fans turned to watch, startled.

"Zebra," the blonde said excitedly, "you are wonderful! I shall report this to Able with my highest recommendations. And do you know what we are going to do now?"

"Uh . . . no sir," he stammered, taken aback.

"Don't sir me," she reproved him. "The name is Dog. And until I am recalled to duty, the name is Mrs. Horace Reid."

Photographic equipment now in everyday use can produce startling results that were only dreams, or science fiction plots, a decade or two ago. One camera uses a radarlike device to focus its lens-train on the subject, while another uses heat-sensitive film to take pictures of the spot where tanks or automobiles were parked several hours ago. The dirtier applications of those two inventions will be along in a few years.

Cameras mounted on high-flying spy planes have taken pictures of a man's footprints on the ground below, and of a pack of cigarettes in that man's shirt pocket. The orbiting spy satellites regularly photograph much more than mere rocket exhausts or above-ground explosions, and when was the last time you were indiscreet while lying on some grassy hillside?

What Pentagon bureaucrat has your picture?

TIME EXPOSURES

SERGEANT TABBOT CLIMBED THE STAIRS TO THE woman's third floor apartment. The heavy camera case banged against his leg as he climbed and threatened collision with his bad knee. He shifted the case to his left hand and muttered under his breath: the woman *could* have been gracious enough to die on the first floor.

A patrolman loafed on the landing, casually guarding the stairway and the third floor corridor.

Tabbot showed surprise. "No keeper? Are they still working in there? Which apartment is it?"

The patrolman said: "Somebody forgot the keeper, Sergeant—somebody went after it. There's a crowd in there, the coroner ain't done yet. Number 33." He glanced down at the bulky case. "She's pretty naked."

"Shall I make you a nice print?"

"No, *sir,* not this one! I mean, she's naked but she ain't pretty anymore."

Tabbot said: "Murder victims usually lose their good looks." He walked down the corridor to number 33 and found the door ajar. A rumbling voice was audible. Tabbot swung the door open and stepped into the woman's apartment. A small place: probably only two rooms.

The first thing he saw was a finger man working over a glass-topped coffee table with an aerosol can and a portable blacklight; the sour expression on the man's face revealed a notable lack of fingerprints. A precinct Lieutenant stood just beyond the end of the coffee table, watching the roving blacklight with an air of unruffled patience; his glance flickered at Tabbot, at the camera case, and dropped again to the table. A plainclothesman waited behind the door, doing nothing. Two men with a wicker basket sat on either arm of an overstuffed chair, peering over the back of the chair at something on the floor. One of them swung his head to stare at the newcomer and then turned his attention back to the floor. Well beyond the chair a bald-headed man wearing too much fat under his clothing was brushing dust from the knees of his trousers. He had just climbed to his feet and the exertion caused a dry, wheezy breathing through an open mouth.

Tabbot knew the Lieutenant and the coroner.

The coroner looked at the heavy black case Tabbot put down just inside the door and asked: "Pictures?"

"Yes, sir. Time exposures."

"I'd like to have prints, then. Haven't seen a shooting in eight or nine years. Damned rare anymore." He pointed a fat index finger at the thing on the floor. "*She* was shot to death. Can you imagine that? Shot to death in *this* day and age! I'd like to have prints. Want to see a man with the gall to carry a gun."

"Yes, sir." Tabbot swung his attention to the precinct Lieutenant. "Can you give me an idea?"

"It's still hazy, sergeant," the officer answered. "The victim knew her assailant; I think she let him in the door and then walked away from him. He stood where you're standing. Maybe an argument, but no fighting—nothing broken, nothing disturbed, no fingerprints. That knob behind you was wiped clean. She was standing behind that chair when she was shot, and she fell there. Can you catch it all?"

"Yes, sir, I think so. I'll set up in that other room—in the doorway. A kitchen?"

"Kitchen and shower. This one is a combination living room and bedroom."

"I'll start in the doorway and then move in close. Nothing in the kitchen?"

"Only dirty dishes. No floorstains, but I would appreciate prints just the same. The floors are clean everywhere except behind *that* chair."

Sergeant Tabbot looked at the window across the room and looked back to the Lieutenant.

"No fire escape," the officer said. "But cover it anyway, cover everything. Your routine."

Tabbot nodded easily, then took a strong grip on his stomach muscles. He moved across the room to the overstuffed chair and peered carefully over the back of it. The two wicker basket men turned their heads in unison to watch him, sharing some macabre joke between them. It would be at his expense. His stomach plunged despite the rigid effort to control it.

She was a sandy blonde and had been about thirty years old; her face had been reasonably attractive but was not likely to have won a beauty contest; it was scrubbed clean, and free of makeup. There was no jewelry on her fingers, wrists, or about her neck; she was literally naked. Her chest had been blown away. Tabbot blinked his shocked surprise and looked down her stomach toward her legs simply to move his gaze away from the hideous sight. He thought for a moment he'd lose his breakfast. His eyes closed while he fought for iron control, and when they opened again he was looking at old abdominal scars from a long ago pregnancy.

Sergeant Tabbot backed off rapidly from the chair and bumped into the coroner. He blurted: "She was shot in the back!"

"Well, of course." The wheezing fat man stepped around him with annoyance. "There's a *little* hole in the spine. Little going in and big—bigod it was big—coming out. Destroyed the rib cage coming out. That's natural. Heavy caliber pistol, I think." He stared down at the naked feet protruding from behind the chair. "*First* shooting I've seen in eight or nine years. Can you imagine that? Somebody carrying a gun." He paused for a wheezing breath and then pointed the same fat finger at the basket men. "Pick it up and run, boys. We'll do an autopsy."

Tabbot walked out to the kitchen.

The kitchen table showed him a dirty plate, coffee cup, fork and spoon, and toast crumbs. A sugar bowl without a lid and a small jar of powdered coffee creamer completed the setting. He looked under the table for the missing knife and butter.

"It's not there," the Lieutenant said. "She liked her toast dry."

Tabbot turned. "How long ago was breakfast? How long has she been dead?"

"We'll have to wait on the coroner's opinion for that but I would guess three, maybe four hours ago. The coffee pot was cold, the body was cold, the egg stains were dry—oh, say three hours plus."

"That gives me a good margin," Tabbot said. "If it happened last night, yesterday, I'd just pick up my camera and go home." He glanced through the doorway at a movement caught in the corner of the eye and found the wicker basket men carrying their load through the front door into the corridor. His glance quickly swung back to the kitchen table. "Eggs and dry toast, sugar in white coffee. That doesn't give you much."

The Lieutenant shook his head. "I'm not worried about *her;* I don't give a damn what she ate. Let the coroner worry about her breakfast; he'll tell us how long ago she ate it and we'll take it from there. Your prints are more important. I want to see pictures of the assailant."

Tabbot said: "Let's hope for daylight, and let's hope it was *this* morning. Are you sure that isn't yesterday's breakfast? There's no point in setting up the camera if it happened yesterday morning, or last night. My exposure limit is between ten and fourteen hours—and you know how poor fourteen-hour prints are."

"This morning," the officer assured him. "She went in to work yesterday morning but when she failed to check in this morning, when she didn't answer the phone, somebody from the shop came around to ask why."

"Did the somebody have a key?"

"No, and that eliminated the first suspect. The janitor let him in. Will you make a print of the door to corroborate their story? A few minutes after nine o'clock; they can't remember the exact time now."

"Will do. What kind of a shop? What did she do?"

"Toy shop. She made Christmas dolls."

Sergeant Tabbot considered that. After a moment he said: "The first thing that comes to mind is toy guns."

The Lieutenant gave him a tight, humorless grin. "We had the same thing in mind and sent men over there to comb the shop. Black market things, you know, toys or the real article. But no luck. They haven't made anything resembling a gun since the Dean Act was passed. That shop was clean."

"You've got a tough job, Lieutenant."

"I'm waiting on your prints, Sergeant."

Tabbot thought that a fair hint. He went back to the outer room and found everyone gone but the silent plainclothesman. The detective sat down on the sofa behind the coffee table and watched him unpack the case. A tripod was set up about five feet from the door. The camera itself was a heavy, unwieldly instrument and was lifted onto the tripod with a certain amount of hard grunting and a muttered curse because of a nipped finger. When it was solidly battened to the tripod, Tabbot picked a film magazine out of the supply case and fixed it to the rear of the camera. A lens and the timing instrument was the last to be fitted into place. He looked to make sure the lens was clean.

Tabbot focused on the front door, and reached into a pocket for his slide rule. He checked the time *now* and then calculated backward to obtain four exposures at nine o'clock, nine-five, nine-ten, and nine-fifteen, which should pretty well bracket the arrival of the janitor and the toy shop employee. He cocked and tripped the timer, and then checked to make sure the nylon film was feeding properly after each exposure. The data for each exposure was jotted down in a notebook, making the later identification of the prints more certain.

The plainclothesman broke his stony silence. "I've never seen one of those things work before."

Tabbot said easily: "I'm taking pictures from nine o'clock to nine-fifteen this morning; if I'm in luck I'll catch the janitor opening the door. If I'm not in luck I'll catch only a blurred movement—or nothing at all—and then I'll have to go back and make an exposure for each minute after nine until I find him. A blurred image of the moving door will pinpoint him."

"*Good* pictures?" He seemed skeptical.

"At nine o'clock? Yes. There was sufficient light coming in that window at nine and not too much time has elapsed. Satisfactory conditions. Things get sticky when I try for night exposures with no more than one or two lamps lit; that simply isn't enough light. I wish *everything* would happen outdoors at noon on a bright day—and not more than an hour ago!"

The detective grunted and inspected the ticking camera. "I took some of your pictures into court once. Bank robbery case, last year. The pictures were bad and the judge threw them out and the case collapsed."

"I remember them," Tabbot told him. "And I apologize for the poor job. Those prints were made right at the time limit: fourteen hours, perhaps a little more. The camera and the film are almost useless beyond ten or twelve hours —that is simply too *much* elapsed time. I use the very best film available but it can't find or make a decent image more than twelve hours in the past. Your bank prints were nothing more than grainy shadows; that's all I can get from twelve to fourteen hours."

"Nothing over fourteen hours?"

"Absolutely nothing. I've tried, but nothing." The camera stopped ticking and shut itself off. Tabbot turned it on the tripod and aimed at the sofa. The detective jumped up.

The sergeant protested. "Don't get up—you won't be in the way. The lens won't see you *now*."

"I've got work to do," the detective muttered. He flipped a dour farewell gesture at the Lieutenant and left the apartment, slamming the door behind him.

"He's still sore about those bank pictures," the officer said.

Tabbot nodded agreement and made a single adjustment on the timing mechanism. He tripped the shutter for one exposure and then grinned at the Lieutenant.

"I'll send him a picture of himself sitting there three minutes ago. Maybe that will cheer him up."

"Or make him mad enough to fire you."

The sergeant began another set of calculations on the slide rule and settled himself down to the routine coverage of the room from six to nine o'clock in the morning. He angled the heavy camera at the coffee table, the kitchen doorway, the overstuffed chair, the window behind the chair, a smaller chair and a bookcase in the room, the floor, a vase of artificial flowers resting on a tiny shelf above a radiator, a floor lamp, a ceiling light, and eventually worked around the room in a circle before coming back to the front door. Tabbot rechecked his calculations and then lavished a careful attention on the door and the space beside it where *he* had stood when he first entered.

The camera poked and pried and peered into the recent past, into the naked blonde's last morning alive, recording on nylon film those images now three or four hours gone. During the circle coverage—between the bookcase and the vase of artificial flowers—a signal light indicated an empty film magazine, and the camera paused in its work until a new magazine was fixed in place. Tabbot made a small adjustment on the timer to compensate for lost time. He numbered the old and the new film magazines, and continued his detailed notes for each angle and series of exposures. The camera ignored the present and probed into the past.

The Lieutenant asked: "How much longer?"

"Another hour for the preliminaries; I can do the kitchen in another hour. And, say, two to three hours for the retakes after something is pinned down."

"I've got work piling up." The officer scratched the back of his neck and then bent down to peer into the lens. "I guess you can find me at the precinct house. Make extra copies of the key prints."

"Yes, sir."

The Lieutenant turned away from his inspection of the lens and gave the room a final, sweeping glance. He did not slam the door behind him as the detective had done.

The full routine of photographing went on.

Tabbot moved the camera backward into the kitchen doorway to gain a broader coverage of the outer room; he angled at the sofa, the overstuffed chair, and again the door. He wanted the vital few moments when the door was opened and the murderer stepped through it to fire the prohibited pistol. Changing to a wide-angle lens, he caught the entire room in a series of ten minute takes over a period of three hours. The scene was thoroughly documented.

He changed magazines to prepare for the kitchen.

A wild notion stopped his hand, stopped him in the act of swiveling the camera. He walked over to the heavy chair, walked around behind it, sidestepped the spilled blood, and found himself in direct line between door and window. Tabbot looked out of the window—imagining a gun at his back—and pivoted slowly to stare at the door: early sunlight coming in the window should have limned the man's face. The camera placed *here* should photograph the assailant's face and record the gun blast as well.

Tabbot hauled tripod and camera across the room and set up in position behind the chair, aiming at the door. The lens was changed again. Another calculation was made. If he was *really* lucky on this series the murderer would fire at the camera.

Kitchen coverage was a near repetition of the first room. It required a little less time.

Tabbot photographed the table and two chairs, the dirty dishes, the toast crumbs, the tiny stove, the aged refrigerator, the tacked-on dish cupboards above the sink and drain board, the sink itself, a cramped water closet masquerading as a broom closet behind a narrow door, and the stained folding door of the shower stall. The stall had leaked.

He opened the refrigerator door and found a half bottle of red wine alongside the foodstuff: two takes an hour apart. He peered into the cramped confines of the water closet: a few desultory exposures, and a hope that the blonde wasn't sitting in there. The shower stall was lined with an artificial white tile now marred by rust stains below a leaky showerhead: two exposures by way of an experiment, because the stall also contained a miniature wash basin, a mirror, and a moisture-proof light fixture. He noted with an absent approval that the fixture lacked a receptacle for plugging in razors.

Tabbot changed to the wide-angle lens for the wrap-up. There was no window in the kitchen, and he made a mental note of the absence of an escape door—a sad violation of the fire laws.

That exhausted the preliminary takes.

Tabbot fished his I.D. card out of his pocket, gathered up the exposed film magazines and walked out of the apartment. There was no keeper blocking passage through the doorway, and he stared with surprise at the patrolman still lounging in the corridor.

The patrolman read his expression.

"It's coming, Sergeant, it's coming. By this time I guess that Lieutenant has chewed somebody out good, so you can bet it's coming in a hurry."

Tabbot put the I.D. card in his pocket.

The patrolman asked: *"Was* she shot up, like they said? Back to front, right out the belly?"

Tabbot nodded uneasily. "Back to front, but out through the rib cage—not the belly. Somebody used a very heavy gun on her. *Do* you want a print? You could paste it up on your locker."

"Oh, hell no!" The man glanced down the corridor and came back to the sergeant. "I heard the coroner say it was a professional job; only the pro's are crazy enough to tote guns anymore. The risk and everything."

"I suppose so; I haven't heard of an amateur carrying one for years. That mandatory jail sentence for possession scares the hell out of them." Tabbot shifted the magazines to his other hand to keep them away from his bad knee going down the stairs.

The street was bright with sunlight—the kind of brilliant

scene which Sergeant Tabbot wanted everything to happen in for better results. Given a bright sun he could reproduce images a little better than grainy shadows, right up to that fourteen-hour stopping point.

His truck was the only police vehicle parked at the curb.

Tabbot climbed into the back and closed the door behind him. He switched on the developing and drying machine in total darkness, and began feeding the film from the first magazine down into the tanks. When the tail of that film slipped out of the magazine and vanished, the leader of the second film was fed into the slot. The third followed when its time came. The sergeant sat down on a stool, waiting in the darkness until the developer and dryer had completed their cycles and delivered the nylon negatives into his hands. After a while he reached out to switch on the printer, and then did nothing more than sit and wait.

The woman's exploded breast hung before his eyes; it was more vivid in the darkness of the truck than in bright daylight. This time his stomach failed to churn, and he supposed he was getting used to the memory. Or the sight-memory was safely in his past. A few of the coming prints *could* resurrect that nightmare image.

The coroner believed some hood had murdered the woman who made Christmas dolls—some professional thug who paid as little heed to the gun law as he did to a hundred and one other laws. Perhaps—and perhaps not. Discharged servicemen were still smuggling weapons into the country, when coming in from overseas posts; he'd heard of that happening often enough, and he'd seen a few of the foolhardy characters in jails. For some reason he didn't understand, ex-Marines who'd served in China were the most flagrant offenders: they outnumbered smugglers from the other services three or four to one and the harsh penalties spelled out in the Dean Act didn't deter *them* worth a damn. Congress in its wisdom had proclaimed that only peace officers, and military personnel on active duty, had the privilege of carrying firearms; all other weapons must under the law be surrendered and destroyed.

Tabbot didn't own a gun; he had no use for one. That patrolman on the third floor carried a weapon, and the Lieutenant, and the plainclothesman—but he didn't think the coroner would have one. Nor the basket men. The Dean Act made stiff prison sentences mandatory for possession among the citizenry, but the Marines kept on carrying them and now and then some civilian died under gunfire. Like the woman who made Christmas dolls.

A soft buzzer signaled the end of the developer's job. Tabbot removed the three reels of nylon negative from the drying rack and fed them through the printer. The waiting time was appreciably shorter. Three long strips of printed pictures rolled out of the printer into his hands. Tabbot didn't waste time cutting the prints into individual frames. Draping two of the strips over a shoulder, he carried the third to the door of the truck and flung it open. Bright sunlight made him squint, causing his eyes to water.

Aloud: "Oh, what the hell! What went wrong?"

The prints were dark, much darker than they had any right to be. He *knew* without rechecking the figures in his notebook that the exposures had been made after sunrise, but still the prints were dark. Tabbot stared up the front of the building, trying to pick out the proper window, then brought his puzzled gaze back to the strip prints. The bedroom-living room was dark.

Peering closer, squinting against the bright light of the sun: four timed exposures of the front door, with the dim figures of the janitor and another man standing openmouth on the third exposure. Ten minutes after nine. The fifth frame: a bright clear picture of the plainclothesman sitting on the sofa, talking up to Tabbot. The sixth frame and onward: dark images of the sofa opened out into a bed—coffee table missing—the kitchen doorway barely discernible, the overstuffed chair (and *there* was the coffee table beside it), the window— He stared with dismay at the window. The goddam drapes were drawn, shutting out the early light!

Tabbot hurriedly checked the second strip hanging on his shoulder: equally dark. The floor lamp and the ceiling light were both unlit. The drapes had been closed all night and the room was in cloudy darkness. He could just identify the radiator, the vase of flowers, the bookcase, the smaller chair, and numerous exposures of the closed door. The floor frames were nearly black. Now the camera changed position, moving to the kitchen doorway and shooting back into the bedroom with a wide-angle lens. Dark frustration.

The bed was folded away into an ordinary sofa, the coffee table had moved back to its rightful position, the remaining pieces of furniture were undisturbed, the drapes covered the only window, the lights were not lit. He squinted at the final frames and caught his breath. A figure —a dim and indistinct somebody of a figure—stood at the far corner of the coffee table looking at the closed door.

Tabbot grabbed up the third strip of prints.

Four frames gave him nothing but a closed door. The fifth frame exploded in a bright halo of flash: the gun was fired into the waiting lens.

Sergeant Tabbot jumped out of the truck, slammed shut the door behind him and climbed the stairs to the third floor. His bad knee begged for an easier pace. The young patrolman was gone from his post upstairs.

A keeper blocked the door to the apartment.

Tabbot approached it cautiously while he fished in his pockets for the I.D. card. At a distance of only two feet he detected the uneasy squirmings of pain in his groin; if he attempted to squeeze past the machine into the apartment the damned thing would do its utmost to tear his guts apart. The testicles were most vulnerable. A keeper always reminded him of a second generation fire hydrant— but if he was grilled at one of the precinct houses he would never be able to describe a second generation fire hydrant to anyone's satisfaction. His interrogator would insist it was only a phallic symbol.

The keeper was fashioned of stainless steel and colorless plastic: it stood waist high with a slot and a glowing bullseye in its pointed head, and it generated a controlled fulguration emission—a high-frequency radiation capable of destroying animal tissue. The machines were remarkably useful for keeping prisoners *in* and inquisitive citizenry *out*.

Tabbot inserted his I.D. into the slot and waited for the glow to fade out of the bullseye.

A telephone rested on the floor at the far end of the sofa, half hidden behind a stack of dusty books: the woman had read Western novels. He dialed the precinct house and waited while an operator located the officer.

Impatiently: "Tabbot here. Who opened the drapes?"

"What the hell are you— What drapes?"

"The drapes covering the window, the only window in the room. Who opened them this morning? When?"

There was a speculative silence. "Sergeant, are those prints worthless?"

"Yes, sir—nearly so. I've got one beautiful shot of that detective sitting on the sofa *after* the drapes were opened."

He hesitated for a moment while he consulted the note-book. "The shot was fired at six forty-five this morning; the janitor opened the door at ten minutes after nine. And I really have a nice print of the plainclothesman."

"Is that *all?*"

"All that will help you. I have one dim and dirty print of a somebody looking at the door, but I can't tell you if that somebody is man or woman, red or green."

The Lieutenant said: "Oh, shit!"

"Yes, sir."

"The coroner opened those drapes—he wanted more light to look at his corpse."

Wistfully: "I wish he'd opened them last night before she was a corpse."

"Are you *sure* they're worthless?"

"Well, sir, if you took them into court and drew that same judge, he'd throw you out."

"Damn it! What are you going to do now?"

"I'll go back to six forty-five and work around that gun-shot. I should be able to follow the somebody to the door at the same time—I suppose it was the woman going over to let the murderer in. But don't get your hopes up, Lieu-tenant. This is a lost cause."

Another silence, and then: "All right, do what you can. A hell of a note, Sergeant."

"Yes, sir." He rang off.

Tabbot hauled the bulky camera into position at one end of the coffee table and angled at the door; he thought the set-up would encompass the woman walking to the door, opening it, turning to walk away, and the assailant coming in. All in murky darkness. He fitted a fresh magazine to the camera, inspected the lens for non-existent dirt, and began the timing calculations. The camera began ticking off the exposures bracketing the point of gunfire.

Tabbot went over to the window to finish his inspection of the third strip of prints: the kitchen. The greater bulk of them were as dark as the bedroom.

The strip of prints suddenly brightened just after that point at which he'd changed to a wide-angle lens, just after he'd begun the final wrap-up. A ceiling light had been turned on in the kitchen.

Tabbot stared at a naked woman seated at the table.

She held both hands folded over her stomach, as though pressing in a roll of flesh. Behind her the narrow door of the water closet stood ajar. The table was bare. Tabbot frowned at the woman, at the pose, and then rummaged through his notes for the retroactive exposure time: five minutes past six. The woman who made Christmas dolls was sitting at a bare table at five minutes past six in the morning, looking off to her left, and holding her hand over her stomach. Tabbot wondered if she were hungry—wondered if she waited on some imaginary maid to prepare and serve breakfast. Eggs, coffee, dry toast.

He searched for a frame of the stove: there was a low gas flame beneath the coffee pot. No eggs frying. Well . . . they were probably three-minute eggs, and these frames had been exposed five or ten minutes apart.

He looked again at the woman and apologized for the poor joke: she would be dead in forty minutes.

The only other item of interest on the third strip was a thin ribbon of light under the shower curtain. Tabbot skipped backward along the strip seeking the two exposures angled into the shower stall, but found them dark and the stall empty. The wrong hour.

Behind him the camera shut itself off and called for attention.

Tabbot carried the instrument across the room to an advantageous position beside an arm of the chair and again angled toward the door. The timer was reset for a duplicate coverage of the scenes just completed, but he expected no more than a shadowy figure entering, firing, leaving—a murky figure in a darkened room. A new series was started with that one flash frame as the centerpiece.

His attention went back to the woman at the table. She sat with her hands clapsed over her stomach, looking off to her left. Looking at what?

On impulse, Tabbot walked into the kitchen and sat down in her chair. Same position, same angle. Tabbot pressed his hands to his stomach and looked off to his left. Identical line of sight. He was looking at the shower stall.

One print had given him a ribbon of light under the stained curtain—no, stained folding door. The barrier had leaked water.

He said aloud: "Well, I'll be damned!"

The printed strips were stretched across the table to free his hands and then he examined his notebook item by item. Each of the prints had peered into the past at five minutes after six in the morning. Someone took a shower while the woman sat by the table.

Back to the last few frames of the second strip taken from the second magazine: a figure—a dim and indistinct somebody of a figure—stood at the far corner of the coffee table looking at the closed door. Time: six-forty. Five minutes before the shot was fired.

Did the woman simply stand there and wait a full five minutes for a knock on the door? Or did she open it only a moment after the exposure was made, let the man in, argue with him, and die five minutes later behind the chair? Five minutes was time enough for an argument, a heated exchange, a threat, a shot.

Tabbot braced his hand on the table edge.

What happened to the man in the shower? Was he still there—soaking himself for forty minutes—while the woman was gunned down? Or had he come out, dried himself, gulped down breakfast and quit the apartment minutes before the assailant arrived?

Tabbot supplied answers: no, no, no, and maybe.

He jumped up from the chair so quickly it fell over. The telephone was behind the stack of Western novels.

The man answering his call may have been one of the wicker basket men.

"County morgue."

"Sergeant Tabbot here, Photo Section. I've got preliminary prints on that woman in the apartment. She was seated at the breakfast table between six o'clock and six-fifteen. How does that square with the autopsy?"

The voice said cheerfully: "Right on the button, Sergeant. The toast was still there, know what I mean?"

Weakly: "I know what you mean. I'll send over the prints."

"Hey, wait—wait, there's more. She was just a little bit pregnant. Two months, maybe."

Tabbot swallowed. An unwanted image tried to form in his imagination: the autopsy table, a stroke or two of the blade, an inventory of the contents of the stomach— He thrust the image away and set down the telephone.

Aloud, in dismay: "I thought the man in the shower ate breakfast! But he didn't—he didn't." The inoperative phone gave him no answer.

The camera stopped peering into the past.

*   *   *

Tabbot hauled the instrument into the kitchen and set up a new position behind the woman's chair to take the table, stove, and shower stall. The angle would be right over her head. A series of exposures two minutes apart was programmed into the timer with the first frame calculated at six o'clock. The probe began. Tabbot reached around the camera and gathered up the printed strips from the table. The light was better at the window and he quit the kitchen for yet another inspection of the dismal preliminaries.

The front door, the janitor and a second man in the doorway, the bright beauty of a frame with the detective sitting on the sofa, the darkened frames of the sofa pulled out to make a bed—Tabbot paused and peered. Were there one or *two* figures sprawled in the bed? Next: the kitchen doorway, the overstuffed chair, the misplaced coffee table, the window with the closed drapes— All of that. On and on. Dark. But were there one or *two* people in the bed?

And now consider this frame: a dim and indistinct somebody looking at the closed door. Was that somebody actually walking to the door, caught in mid-stride? Was that somebody the man from the shower?

Tabbot dropped the strips and sprinted for the kitchen.

The camera hadn't finished its programmed series but Tabbot yanked it from position and dragged it over the kitchen floor. The tripod left marks. The table was pushed aside. He stopped the timer and jerked aside the folding door to thrust the lens into the shower stall. Angle at the tiny wash basin and the mirror hanging above it; hope for sufficient reflected light from the white tiles. Strap on a fresh magazine. Work feverishly with the slide rule. Check and check again the notes to be certain of times. Set the timer and start the camera. Stand back and wait.

The Lieutenant had been wrong.

The woman who made Christmas dolls did *not* walk to the door and admit a man at about six-forty in the morning; she didn't go to the door at all. She died behind the chair, as she was walking toward the window to pull the drapes. Her assailant had stayed the night, had slept with her in the unfolded bed until sometime shortly before six o'clock. They got up and one of them used the toilet, one of them put away the bed. *He* stepped into the shower while *she* sat down at the table. In that interval she held her belly, and later had breakfast. An argument started—or perhaps was carried over from the night before—and when the man emerged into a now *darkened* kitchen he dressed and made to leave without eating.

The argument continued into the living room; the woman went to the window to admit the morning sun while the professional gunman hesitated between the coffee table and the door. He half turned, fired, and made his escape.

"There's a *little* hole in the spine . . ."

Tabbot thought the Lieutenant was very wrong. In less than an hour he would have the prints to prove him wrong.

To save a few minutes' time he carried the exposed magazine down to the truck and fed the film into the developing tank. It was a nuisance to bother with the keeper each time he went in and out, and he violated regulations by leaving it inert. A police cruiser went by as he climbed down from the truck but he got nothing more than a vacant nod from the man riding alongside the driver. Tabbot's knee began to hurt as he climbed the steps to the third floor for what seemed the hundredth time that day.

The camera had completed the scene and stopped.

Tabbot made ready to leave.

He carried his equipment outside into the corridor and shot three exposures of the apartment door. The process of packing everything back into the bulky case took longer than the unpacking. The tripod stubbornly refused to telescope properly and fit into the case. And the citizens' privacy law stubbornly refused to let him shoot the corridor: no crime there.

A final look at the unoccupied apartment: he could see through into the kitchen and his imagination could see the woman seated at the table, holding her stomach. When he craned his neck to peer around the door he could see the window limned in bright sunshine. Tabbot decided to leave the drapes open. If someone else were killed here today or tomorrow he wanted the drapes open.

He closed the apartment door and thrust his I.D. card into the keeper's slot to activate it. There was no rewarding stir of machinery, no theatrical buzzing of high-frequency pulsing but his guts began growling when the red bullseye glowed. He went down the stairs carefully because his knee warned against a fast pace. The camera case banged his other leg.

Tabbot removed the reel of film from the developing tanks and started it through the printer. The second magazine was fed into the developer. He closed the back door of the truck, went around to the driver's door and fished for the ignition key in his trouser pocket. It wasn't there. He'd left the key hanging in the ignition, another violation of the law. Tabbot got up in the cab and started the motor, briefly thankful the men in the police cruiser hadn't spotted the key—they would have given him a citation and counted him as guilty as any other citizen.

The lab truck moved out into traffic.

The printing of the two reels of nylon film was completed in the parking lot alongside the precinct house. He parked in a visitor's slot. Not knowing who might be watching from a window, Tabbot removed the key from the ignition and pocketed it before going around to the back to finish the morning's work.

The strip results from the first magazine were professionally insulting: dark and dismal prints he didn't really want to show anyone. There were two fine frames of gun flash, and two others of the dim and indistinct somebody making for the door. About the only satisfaction Tabbot could find in these last two was the dark coloring: a man dressed in dark clothing, moving through a darkened room. The naked woman would have been revealed as a pale whitish figure.

Tabbot scanned the prints on the second strip with a keen and professional eye. The white tile lining the shower stall had reflected light in a most satisfying manner: he thought it one of the best jobs of back-lighting he'd ever photographed. He watched the woman's overnight visitor shower, shave, brush his teeth and comb his hair. At one point—perhaps in the middle of that heated argument—he had nicked himself on the neck just above his Adam's apple. It had done nothing to improve the fellow's mood.

One exposure made outside the apartment door—the very last frame—was both rewarding and disappointing: the indistinct somebody was shown leaving the scene but he was bent over, head down, looking at his own feet. Tabbot supposed the man was too shy to be photographed coming out of a woman's room. He would be indignant when he learned that a camera had watched him in the little mirror above the wash basin. Indignant, and rather furious at this newest invasion of privacy.

Tabbot carried the prints into the precinct house. Another sergeant was on duty behind the desk, a man who recognized him by uniform if not by face or name.

"Who do you want?"

Tabbot said: "The Lieutenant. What's-his-name?"

The desk man jerked a thumb behind him. "In the squad room."

Tabbot walked around the desk and found his way to the squad room at the end of the building. It was a large room with desks, and four or five men working or loafing behind the desks. Most of them seemed to be loafing. All of them looked up at the photographer.

"Over here, Sergeant. Did you finish the job?"

"Yes, sir."

Tabbot turned and made his way to the Lieutenant's desk. He spread out the first strip of dark prints.

"Well, you don't seem too happy about it."

"No, sir."

The second strip was placed beside the first.

"They're all dark except those down at the bottom. It was brighter in the shower stall. That's you in the shower, Lieutenant. The backlighting gave me the only decent prints in the lot."

THE BEST AUTHORS. THEIR BEST STORIES.

Pocket Books presents a continuing series of very special collections.

THE BEST OF POUL ANDERSON
____ 83140/$2.25

THE BEST OF DAMON KNIGHT
____ 83375/$2.50

THE BEST OF WALTER M. MILLER, JR.
____ 83304/$2.95

THE BEST OF JACK VANCE
____ 44186/$2.95

THE BEST OF ROBERT SILVERBERG
____ 83497/$2.50

THE BEST OF KEITH LAUMER
____ 83268/$2.25

THE BEST OF JOHN SLADEK
____ 83131/$2.50

232